The Pledge - A Collection of Tales

Wondrous Tales, Volume 1

Viktor F. Krown

Published by Viktor F. Krown, 2024.

THE PLEDGE
A COLLECTION OF TALES

by Viktor F. Krown

Foreword

Lose yourself within the pages of this bizarre collection of fantastic tales. Traverse the realms beyond your wildest dreams.

Each of these tales was originally written in real-time during the Wondrous Tales and was based on the wild ideas and prompts that the audience gave me on that day.

Although each of these stories underwent careful revision and editing to enhance their quality for this printed version, they retain the spirit, essence, and core that made them the beloved and cherished - Wondrous Tales.

This mini-collection was created to commemorate the two-year anniversary of Wondrous Tales, a significant milestone that I am proud and grateful for.

I wish you a pleasant journey through these tales.

- Viktor F. Krown,
author of Wondrous Tales

Archived Feelings

Caden watched a gorgeous female bard playing for a crowd amidst which he found himself. Her hair was as white as winter's first snow. Spanning halfway down her back it was beautifully braided, so as not to get in the way of her plucking the strings of the acoustic guitar. She sat upon a small, foldable stool atop a portable stage. The crowd was remarkably sizeable. At first, she played a slow and steady rhythm, which complemented the story she was telling.

"And then the hero slipped..."

She strummed the strings faster and with more force, changing the rhythm, quickening it - to instill a sense of urgency in the listeners.

"But before he had time to react, something broke his fall and brought him high up into the skies," she continued the tale. With music - a perfect companion, the story felt almost tangible and left the listeners awestruck.

Caden grinned, excited for the continuation of the tale. Her performances were not only captivating, but magical.

The story came to an end. Caden applauded along with the rest of the crowd, tossed a few coins on the stage inconspicuously, and moved on. Something about her genuinely captured his attention every time he got to see her play, and albeit it was infrequent, each time was memorable. She was not only mesmerizing in appearance, but her storytelling reached into his heart as if she was weaving the melody with the strings of his feelings. He had always been a sucker for a good story and her talent for storytelling, in combination with the exceptional bardic skills, made her tales utmost enjoyable for him.

Caden glanced over his shoulder. People were tossing coins into her hat and she was chatting with a few audience members. He pondered for a moment, *'a few coins are not enough... she deserves more, a truly unique gift for her talents. Yes, something special.'*

Shortly after the show she packed her belongings, threw her bags into the magicart behind her, and hopped into the driver's seat. He watched her with a twinkle in his eyes until she disappeared around the corner down the street. A gentle sigh escaped his lips as a thought lingered on his mind. *'Wonder when I'll get to see you again, bard to my heart.'*

"What ye up ta pal? Ain't a place for a kid like ye-self!" spoke a man from the shadows of the dark alley, behind Caden.

Something shimmered in Caden's hand. His friendly smile turned menacing, his hands were a blur. A moment later the wall was painted red, as was the cobble street upon which the fresh corpse lay. He knelt, checked the pockets of the still-warm body, pulled out some documents, ripped a necklace off the chain, and then disappeared into the shadows.

Caden tossed a small, cloth bag onto the reception table of some hotel, then turned and leaned against it.

A man draped in a butler's suit and a monocle - glanced around the empty, midnight lobby, then fixated his gaze on the bag.

"Objective completed; items received. Clean work, Caden?"

Caden nodded. "The body will be discovered tomorrow morning, but no connection to the organization will be made, I made sure of it."

The man in the suit pushed an envelope toward Caden and grabbed the bag.

"Your payment... anything else?"

Caden tilted his head to the side. "What's the... rarest flower in the world?"

The man in the suit turned, putting away a bag that Caden turned in.

"Hmm, I reckon that'd be Meniva," he responded, an undertone of admiration in his voice. "It is rumored that only a dozen of them exist at any one time. An odd question, for a killer. Going on a date?"

Caden shrugged. "Intel's part of the deal, just a side gig, don't worry about what I'll do with it, and thanks, see-ya."

When the dawn broke, he eagerly prepared to learn more about the Meniva flower.

The first stop was the florist. As expected, he knew little about this rare specimen that Caden was after, yet he offered a high price for it, should the rogue bring him one. The visit was not in vain, from the florist Caden learned of a legendary traveling witch - Max, who was supposedly in the area. The florist mentioned that her hut was in the forest just outside the city. His next destination was set, a witch's hut in the forest. There is not anyone who would not know of the legendary traveling witch, the maestro of potion brewing - Max. Caden considered himself lucky to have this opportunity.

When Caden reached her hut and knocked on the door, he was met with a confusing mixture of a pleasantly friendly person who was not what he had expected at all. She was polite, as the rumors suggested, but was not a *she* at all. Before him was an aged, wrinkly man.

"Greetings... uhmm, Mmmmax? I'm looking for the traveling witch by the name of Max."

The man arched his eyebrow. "Max is me, yes, that is I," he smiled warmly and stepped aside, gesturing to the visitor to come in.

"How may I be of assistance? A potion? Charm? Or something more..." he paused, as if at a loss for words, "Maybe, erhm, what's the... ugh, no matter. Would you like a cup of herb-brewery?"

Caden was perplexed. *'Aren't witches implied to be female? What is even the difference between a witch and a wizard? Both use magic, right?'* He pondered over a question that he seemingly never had a reason to ask before. He was a rogue - the magical shenanigans were never something he concerned himself with, it was simply above his pay grade.

"Thanks, but I'll pass on the offer. I seek the most magnificent of all flowers in the world, the Meniva flower. I was told that you - a wise witch...er... Witcher! W...wizard?? Witch... zard... might know of it," he stumbled over his words out of confusion over Max's deceiving appearance, which contradicted his expectations.

"I am Max, a witch, yes," the aged man replied, seemingly lost in thoughts, presumably recollecting what he knew about the flower.

"I thought witches were all female and wizards? Or erhm, I mean witchers, were the male equivalent?"

"Correct! Almost... The wizards are different, they have no natural talent," he replied with a smirk. "Though... that Mineva, doesn't ring a bell."

"No, it's Meniva, not Mineva," Caden corrected the witch.

"Ahh! That makes a difference. I had forgotten what you said, my apologies... my memory isn't quite so good." He finished his herb brewery and got up to collect various ingredients from the nearest shelf. Caden took the opportunity to admire the interior of the witch's hut. It was surprisingly minimalistic but quite homely and welcoming.

Max returned and proceeded to put various ingredients into a mortar. He paused at one point and eyed intently the two eggs that he held in his wrinkly hands. The egg he held in his left hand was much smaller than the right hand's egg, and was whiter in color.

Caden awkwardly cleared his throat in hopes of reacquiring the witch's attention.

"Ahem, so about the flower."

"Yes, I too wonder which egg is right for this potion. A client is coming soon, and I can't recall if it's the snow owl's egg, or the hawk's..." Max's eyes darted between the two eggs.

"Right, the flower... travel far, to the land of Rivera, to the Grand Library of All, and there they should have records of it... maybe... I know no more."

Max dropped the smaller, whiter egg into the mortar and nodded.

"Should be the snow owl's egg... I hope!" His eyes widened as if bewildered by a sudden flash of memories, or a vision.

Whatever was the case, he had no desire to stay long enough to find out. He got up swiftly after noticing the concern in the witch's eyes and headed straight for the door.

"Very well! Thank you for the assistance, Max. If you ever need services of a specialty rogue, just call my name to the shadows three times at New Moon."

Max nodded absentmindedly.

Caden put some distance between him and the hut, climbed upon a watch tower and then pulled out a wallet-like item from his hidden pocket. He pulled out a piece of see-through and spectral-looking paper. A few brief moments later a train's whistle was heard in the distance, approaching fast.

A set of ghost tracks appeared just before him; his position was now a Spectral Express's stop. These unique train tickets cost a literal fortune, but they were worth it. The locomotive could be summoned to almost any location, and at any time of the day. An individual conductor with a private wagon. The train rode upon ghostly tracks and would take you anywhere in the world. It was faster than any other means of transportation, well, except teleportation, but only wizards, witches, witchers, and a handful of special others had that luxury.

A brief moment - before the train came to a halt, a beastly screech shaved a few years off of Caden's life. A colossal shadow eclipsed the sun and rushed past him, heading for the witch's hut. Bewildered by the horrific experience, Caden took a deep breath and then shuddered.

"Get in el'ready, ain't got el' day!" shouted the conductor out of the locomotive's window. The shout snapped Caden out of his stupor, and he boarded at last.

"So much for a magical experience..." Caden grumbled under his breath.

"Get it straight, it's spectral! That's SPEC-TRAL for you! No mere magical mumbo-jumbo here," the conductor corrected him.

The next stop in his search for the flower was the Grand Library. A rather obvious destination on the quest for knowledge, in an extraordinarily abnormal location. Per Max's suggestion, Caden found himself traveling across the continent to the magic-ridden land of Rivera - a journey which took the whole day.

He arrived in Rivera, and after numerous inquiries for directions, he finally found himself in the halls of the Grand Library. The library proved to be far more grandiose than he could have imagined. An occasional book would flutter past him, pursued by an apprentice librarian with a bug net. Wizards walked through walls and on ceilings. Some floors of the library appeared to be twisted and turned ninety degrees. Some parts of it were curled up into a spiral, an endless spiral that seemingly extended inwards endlessly. Clouds indoors somehow seemed normal in a place this bizarre. It was truly a phenomenal place, one he couldn't even dream of. Yet amidst the chaos of magic stood. It was before and above, and all around him. He struggled to believe that such a place existed, or that any of what he was seeing was real. He failed to comprehend almost anything of what he was seeing. None of it made any sense, not logical at least. He was bumfuzzled by the dizzying experience and the mind-boggling sight that was right before his eyes. After moments, or perhaps hours of admiration, he finally mustered enough strength and courage to approach the reception desk.

His inquiry was filed, and he was asked to wait for a librarian guide - who appeared in front of him seemingly out of thin air, as soon as he sat down. It was a girl in purple robes with a nerdy appearance.

"I'm Clare, an archivist," she introduced herself with a sweet tone, omitting any unnecessary details. Her hair was dark, bundled up into a bun, but did not appear to be long. She was average height, but he could hardly tell much about her physique since it was enshrouded by the robes.

She scanned him up and down as he did her. Before herself, she saw a stereotypical rogue assassin. Dark clothes, a hidden dagger that was as obvious as the moon in the night sky, and another one in his boot. His chiseled face was decorated by a stubble and a couple of insignificant scars. His hair was short. She chortled, bemused.

"My, my. I can guess your profession at a single glance. You really ought to hide it better."

Her childish giggle somehow lightened his mood, despite being mesmerized and awestruck by the Grand Library that stretched seemingly endlessly above him, spanning through the clouds, both indoor and outside.

"Hello," he replied, "I'm Caden. I'm looking for..."

She nodded and interrupted him.

"Mhmm. Yes, the Meniva flower. Come with me, records of these rare flowers are stored in the archives. Their rarity makes them somewhat unknown, and knowledge of them is all but obsolete. No one seems to be searching for them anymore," she explained, gesturing for him to follow. "And please refrain from touching anything, especially in the archives where we're headed."

He tilted his head to the side. "That strict?"

She shook her head, guiding him to a circular tile on the floor, then spoke in a language he could not understand. The tile separated from the floor and began to descend into a dark abyss.

"No, rather because it is dangerous."

"How so?" Caden asked while staring into the ever-darkening void into which they were descending.

"In the Grand Library all books, tomes, scrolls, and artifacts are stored in perfect harmony to neutralize each other's effects."

Caden nodded. "So... if one is removed, the harmony is broken."

She nodded, confirming his guess. "And the power of the said tomes can run wild, occasionally resulting in a loose werewolf or a whole new dimension," she shrugged. "So... be careful."

He offered her a nervous smile as a bead of sweat formed on his brow. "Y-yes, noted..."

"Oh, relax! It's not that bad. Our librarians are the best in the world, no, wait, across all the worlds... and realms," she corrected her remark and then gave him a playful chuckle. "Did you know that the library links endless dimensions? Even the almighty Overseer visits us occasionally."

Caden nodded, not grasping half of what she was saying. "Yeah, uhm... so how far down is this?"

The round tile on which they stood came to a sudden stop. A faint glow emerged from it, barely illuminating the dark floor around them. The air was dry and only the scent of old books lingered in the air. When Clare stepped out of the circle, the floor began to glow beneath her, and that gentle glow guided their way, following Clare's every step.

He followed in her footsteps through the dark corridors of the mysterious archives. A question sprung up in his mind amidst the rhythmic echoes of their steps.

"Say, what's the, uhh, difference between mages, wizards, witches, and, uhh, you, the librarians?"

She gasped and turned on her heel instantly, her eyes glistened with excitement, reflecting the dim floor's light in them.

"Oh my god! What a delightfully wonderful and *magical* question. Ohh, where do I even begin?" She almost squealed with excitement.

"Soooooo... wizards are learned, erhm, taught. They learn to use magic through studies and perseverance."

"So does that mean that anyone can become a wizard?"

She shook her head. "No, not quite. It still takes a natural affinity with the winds of magic to be able to control them and weave them to one's desire..." she paused, "imagine magic winds to be like snow, but, some people can't touch it. You need to be able to touch it, to shape it to your will. Still with me?"

"I... mostly. So what are witches and witchers then?"

"Right, they differ vastly from wizards due to their innate *talent* as one might call it. They are basically prodigies from birth. Don't get me wrong! They still need to study, but due to their inborn talent in control of magic, they instead focus their time studying alchemy, chemistry, and herbology." She paused and took a deep breath, having run out of air while enthusiastically explaining, and continued. "That's why so many refer to them as brewers and alchemists, they're incredibly well-versed in the herbal brewery and such! Unlike wizards.... who focus their studies on magical theory and control - since they lack that natural born *feel* for magic, well... that is the short version at least."

"Oh, so they do not *feel* magic, they just understand it and use it?"

"Precisely! But that is also why you don't see witchcraft prodigies create new spells."

She glanced up at the ceiling, "This here library is full of spell makers in fact. They're wizards whose understanding of magical theory is above all others. They can create new spells by figuring out how to shape the winds of magic to their will, and force it to do their bidding."

"Aha..."

"Most witches and witchers do not have that in-depth understanding, they simply feel the magic and get a grasp on spells that are of interest to them."

"So, why not both?"

"Why *not* indeed," she remarked teasingly. "They exist, you know? And they're terrifying. Some call them *Supreme Sorcerers,* others dub them - the *Grand Wizards.* They go by many names, but essentially, they're the ones with both - the understanding, and the natural talent to go along with it. Truly frightening, if you ask me," she remarked with a sly grin, "but oh so fascinating. You should meet one someday."

"Uhh, no I... uhm, I think I'm good."

They passed through an aisle of books with shelves shorter than most others and seemed a little disorganized. Thoughts bubbled up in his wandering mind: *'The Grand Library's archives - secret knowledge stowed away and hidden from the world. Mysteries untold, enshrouded by the darkness of the underground. It could be anything. Each of these books, in theory, is priceless.'* A grin spread on his face and his instincts stirred.

He glanced around to confirm that it was just him and Clare in these empty archives, or at least in the proximity. As far as he could tell, there did not appear to be any surveillance devices around. The rhythmic echoes of their steps would serve as a concealment for any subtle noises he might make. *'Do it...'*

With each step, his eagerness and excitement grew. His gaze fixated on a book on a shelf a few paces ahead. It was a little smaller than the others, with a faded lilac cover. Most importantly, it protruded out of the line ever so slightly, as if begging to be snatched. He gulped quietly, swallowing the lump of nervousness in his throat. Then, unbuttoned his coat in preparation for theft. Each step brought him closer to his target. When the book was in the line of his shoulder, in a swift sleight of hand the book was now in his possession, and a short shuffle of cloth later, it was safely tucked away in the inner pocket of his coat.

The books beside the one he snatched buzzed for a moment, and then abruptly fell silent. He walked on as if nothing had happened, trying to calm his heart, which was drumming in his chest from thrill and adrenaline. Clare seemed oblivious to the bold act of thievery that took place right behind her.

She gestured towards a reading table in a dark corner, offering him a seat.

"Please wait here, I'll fetch the tomes that should have details on the flower."

He nodded and took the offered seat. As she disappeared into the shadows, he seized the opportunity and peeked at the book he had snatched earlier - a worn tome, the title of which read: *Cooking Rocks with Actual Rocks*.

He squinted at it, muttering a quiet and confused, "The fu..." as he flipped it open, he read over one of the recipes.

Caramel-Glazed Rocks

Collect coin-sized pebbles, smoothed by the river

Melt sugar in a pot

Remember to cook on low heat

Then toss in the pebbles

Increase heat slowly and continue stirring in clockwise direction, unless you're in the Northern Hemisphere, then stir in counterclockwise direction.

Make sure to flip the pebbles every five minutes, three times

When all pebbles have undergone three flips, remove from fire and let cool under fresh air, with winds no stronger than 10 km/h

Enjoy cold or heated

The caramelized pebbles also make for a great appetizer

He blinked in disbelief and flipped through the book, glancing through the other recipes briefly. They were not much different; they were indeed cooking recipes using, seemingly. actual rocks, but also sand, crystals, and other variations of solid earth materials, some even including the use of metal.

Shortly after, she returned with the tomes, and they examined them together. Though, it was mostly Clare who was taking notes as she read about the flower.

"There's... half a page is missing..." she pointed out while examining the tome. "How peculiar... I'll need a temporal wizard." She scribbled notes of this in her notebook and then shifted her focus back to the client's research request to finish it up.

Meanwhile, Caden was mostly spacing out and dozing off in the chair next to hers. When all was done, she presented him with a hand-drawn map, pointing to the Southern peaks.

"Southern peaks?" He examined the map while sleepily rubbing his eyes.

She smiled. "Mhmm, as I previously noted, practically nobody looks for those flowers anymore. Good luck," she remarked with a hint of sarcasm.

She swiftly got rid of the rogue by guiding him to the nearest exit and set off to have the damaged tome repaired. Time was of the essence, literally - for she needed a temporal wizard for the fix.

He walked outside, down the cobblestone streets. It was early morning, and the rising sun pleasantly warmed his skin - a welcomed sensation after spending the night in the musty, dark, library's archive. However, to him, the place had a homely atmosphere and reminded him of his teen years. Now that he was out on the streets again, he was beginning to miss it a little. Yet his yearning to return was pushed aside by a pleasant and familiar melody that caught his attention, a tune he thought he recognized. He rounded the corner from where the melody echoed, and there she was: sitting on her stool, guitar firmly in her hands, eyes closed - telling a story once more, to the rhythm of her guitar's gentle tones.

A small crowd began to gather around her. She slowly reopened her eyes when Caden's gaze fell upon her, and the music abruptly stopped. She gasped, "What? Where am I?" Shocked and disturbed, she scanned the crowd and the scenery around her for anything familiar, but nothing was recognizable to her. Her concerned gaze fluttered past Caden a few times, seemingly unaware that she had seen him before. He blended surprisingly well into the throng, despite his rather peculiar outfit.

Concern and nervousness were still obvious on her face, but an audience had already gathered, and she, being the performer she was, resumed her show. The bard wove a tale as captivating as all her others. It was a tragic story of a space-faring crew that landed on a planet of fey, but never made it out; for the fey were anything but friendly.

After the performance, she frantically scanned the crowd once again. Her gaze fell on Caden, the only one in no rush to leave. He was observing her with morbid curiosity. When their eyes met, she at last gave him her full attention.

"Do... you know me?" she asked curiously, with a guitar in one hand and her belongings in a bag thrown over her shoulder, held by a strap in the other.

He gave her a warm smile. "I've seen you perform before, but it was far from here. What brings you here?"

She shrugged. "How should I know? I was performing. I was in the flow, closed my eyes, and swayed to the rhythm. When I reopened them, I was here." She glanced around and shuddered.

"Welcome to the land of peculiarity and magic, huh?" He took a quick glance around and spotted a café just on the corner, down the street. "Say, how about a warm drink to soothe your uneasiness?" he suggested, already taking a few steps toward the café.

The bard sighed, and the rogue smiled, his gaze fixated on a waiter, who had just served some drinks to people outside, and on the way back inside, he slipped and fell. All three gasped in unison as cups and coffee sailed through the air, accelerating toward the floor. The clatter of spoons and tinkle of broken glass and porcelain made them both squint sympathetically and grit their teeth. For a moment, he thought he heard something else, the sound of a distant explosion. At the Grand Library, something exploded with enough force to kill a goblin lord who had emerged from one of the tomes. This unexpected and unforeseen death caused an effect that rippled through the world. In a kingdom far away, an army of goblins, loyal to the deceased lord, declared war on the Wizard of the Tinfoil Hat. The librarians rushed to extinguish the flames after the explosion, and settle the situation that arose in the archives. Something was amiss, something crucial to the balance of the tomes, was missing.

At the cafe, Caden had returned to the table carrying two cups filled with steaming hot, liquid, not trusting the waiters after the witnessed events. He sat one cup in front of the bard, and the other on the opposite side of the table.

"So, ehem, ever uhm, this ever happened to you before?" Caden asked, obviously nervous.

"You mean suddenly being teleported to the other side of the world? No, can't say that is a common occurrence."

"Yeah..." he mumbled in response.

He took a seat across from her and took a slow and distracted sip of his beverage. His gaze was focused on the woman in front of him, and then he broke the awkward silence with a pained gasp, followed by a loud thud of the cup on the table.

"Aghhh! Mmhh! Mhy tohong!!!"

She watched him with a bemused expression before bursting into laughter.

"You've really ought to be more careful," her voice trailed off into a hushed whisper, "dork..."

"Mmhh?" He inquired as he carefully pressed the cold blade of his dagger on his burned tongue to soothe the burning sensation. At that moment, a waitress approached them with a cup of cold water.

"Are you alright, mister?" she asked with worry in her tone, but her gaze was firmly fixated on the blade of his dagger. A rogue, assassin, killer, thief; his kind was not exactly welcomed here, but as long as he caused no trouble, she had no reason to act any differently toward him.

"Here, better than sucking on a knife," the waitress offered him the cup.

He grabbed it in one swept motion and gulped it down in an instant.

"Ahhh! Better, much better! Thank you kindly!" His gaze darted from the waitress back to the bard of his interests. "Now... did you say something?"

The bard tittered and shook her head.

"No, no. Who are you? You said you've seen me perform before?"

"That's right, uhhh... a handful of times in fact. Hmm, can't quite recall how many, but your stories! And your music! So captivating and mesmerizing!"

She looked to the side, rosy-cheeked.

"Oh please. I'm not that great. I just retell stories I hear and read, and add a bit of rhythm to them."

"No, you're not great indeed, you're the *greatest*!" he insisted, protesting her remark.

Her blush grew brighter. "Well, thank you kindly for the sweet words."

"So, uhm, do you..."

"Where are we?" she inquired, interrupting his train of thought.

"A, uhh, café...?"

"No! Yes, I get that. I mean here, where is this place exactly on the world map?"

"Ah, we're in Rivera."

She let out a gasp and stared out the window, a shadow of a witch on a broom slithered past them.

"Oh no," she whispered under her breath.

"Huh? W... what's wrong?"

She snapped her attention back to him, then rested her cheek on the palm of her hand, giving him the sweetest smile he had ever seen. With her other hand she rhythmically drummed on the table.

"Oh, it's nothing. I just have a performance in a few days, and it would seem I won't make it back in time, and... I've no money on me to get back."

His heart pounded, his mind went blank, all he could think about was her, a damsel in distress, *a perfect opportunity*, he thought.

"I will try to, uhm, get you back on time." He scratched the back of his head and pondered for a minute.

"Will do my damndest to get you back in time for your performance, but there's something I've to do first. Will you wait a day or couple?" His eyes darted between her silvery eyes, like two perfect moons on a clear starry night, stared right back at him. As if cornered by a predator, he felt anxious, pressured, and spoke without thinking.

"And don't worry about money. I'll get you a room and cover the expenses." He winked at her, attempting his best to hide his anxiousness.

"Oh! No! No no no! You cannot do that. That would be unfair."

He picked up his cup and took a cautious sip, then sat it back down and smirked.

"It's the least I can do for my favorite storyteller."

"Mmmhhh..." she frowned slightly, "and how do I repay you then?"

He glanced up at the ceiling, thinking about it. His desires and interests clearly conflicted with his mannerisms. "A smile will do."

She raised an eyebrow and snickered.

"Dork..." A sweet smile spread across her lips. "I'll prepare a special story just for you, my... hero..."

His heart skipped a beat and he excitedly jumped up from his chair. "I! Will be right back! And then we'll get you situated at the inn!" He rushed off.

Upon his return, they headed to the inn and got her situated in a room that would be her home for the foreseeable few days while she awaited his return.

Caden departed on his quest to acquire the rare flower that he felt would be a worthy gift for the bard he so admired. He used one of his two remaining Spectral Express tickets and summoned the train just outside the city to take him to the Southern peaks. His mind was filled with concerns. Sure, finding himself in the wilderness was nothing too out of the ordinary for a rogue, however, mountain climbing was far outside his comfort zone and area of expertise. He was far more comfortable sneaking through windows, pickpocketing, and parkouring around on rooftops. Nevertheless, his feelings and desires pushed him forth. She was waiting for him, and he thought that returning with such a unique and rare gift would likely cause her to smile. He longed to see her smile.

Hours passed and turned into days of relentless onslaught from the elements. He faced off against blizzards and endured the biting winds that assaulted him with icy needles. After enduring two days and three nights of starvation and relentless attack, he finally rejoiced at last. He stood on the lush green grass at the summit of the fourth peak that he had conquered in those few, agonizing days.

Bright, blinding light enveloped the horizon, there was nothing to see from the peak but whiteness. The grass's greenery was interrupted only by sporadic golden flowers that emitted a faint glow. An echo of a voice disturbed the peace he found at last. It came from everywhere and nowhere at the same time. The voice came from the land, every blade of grass, and the air itself, but also from inside his head. He thought he had gone mad from hunger and fever, but the voice brought a sense of tranquility and comfort with it.

"Beautiful, are they not?" it spoke.

His eyes shot open when he saw a figure in black robes sitting by one of the glowing flowers. A fascinating contrast of the pitch-black robes, green grass, golden-glowing flowers, and endless whiteness that surrounded it all.

Caden reached for his dagger, weary of the stranger he had encountered and the voice he had heard. The voice echoed through the lands and his mind alike once more.

"No need, I am merely here to admire."

The figure rose to standing height, and then vanished from existence.

Caden let out a relaxed sigh, uncertain whether the encountered figure was a figment, a deity, or one of the grand wizards that the archivist had mentioned, but it hardly concerned him - his goal was in his sights. The flowers he sought after resembled wheat in shape but not in size. He approached one carefully and knelt beside it, his trembling finger brushed its stalk. The surrounding grass pulsed and swayed, as if reacting to his touch.

With a swift sleight of hand and a determined mind, he drew his dagger and sliced through the flower's stem. Its glow became brighter than before, but in that instant, the grass around it withered. A dry patch of grass now contrasted the beautiful, lush green that was engulfed by the blinding whiteness, creating a strange but somehow beautiful symphony of colors.

Having obtained what he had come for, he thought for a moment about gathering another flower, or even all the remaining flowers, of which there were barely half a dozen. He contemplated, but then shook his head, deciding against it after taking one more glance at the dry patch of grass. He had no need for money. '*Greed only brings troubles,*' he reminded himself, and used his distinguished and rare VIP ticket to summon the Spectral Express. Upon its arrival, he requested a stop at Rivera to pick up his dear bard who was awaiting his return.

The conductor glanced over the company policies booklet and read the policy for the VIP tickets: '*The customer is always right because they pay us a lot of money! So do as they say, so long as it is sensible.*' After reading it, he reluctantly complied with the request and plotted a new course. "Ble'dy VEEPS," he grumbled.

Ghostly tracks spanned the air, and the train carried him effortlessly back to Rivera to meet his beloved bard, whose name he still did not know, and forgot to ask. The train came to a screeching halt just outside the city. He now had exactly one hour to find his beloved and reboard before the allotted waiting interval expired, and the train would depart with or without the VIP passenger and his plus one.

With the glowing flower wrapped in cloth and stashed in his pouch, he hurried to the inn, but the bard was nowhere to be found. The innkeeper told him that she had stepped out with her guitar, so he had no choice but to roam the streets of Rivera in search of her.

He walked fast, traversing the streets of an unfamiliar to him city. Someone fell off a broom behind him. Caden ignored it, he had no time to waste, and plenty of good-willed people rushed to their aid. Off to the side, Caden overheard a middle-aged woman, who was watering flowers outside of what he assumed was her flower shop. She sounded perplexed, as if questioning reality. "What in the frosted over hell is going on with this thing?"

"What happened?" asked a young man who was looking at the flowers, of the florist.

"This blasted thing won't water anymore." A magical watering can suddenly ran out of water, leaving the florist baffled as Caden passed by.

A frog leaped onto the street just a few paces ahead of him. Suddenly it transformed into a man who then awkwardly ribbited at Caden before darting off into the alley, desperately trying to cover his private parts.

"Uhuh..." Caden puzzled, "I wonder if this is considered normal around here." He hastened his pace in hopes of finding the bard sooner. Abnormalities kept happening, and yet he remained focused on the task at hand, listening intently; not to the chaos that was unfolding around him, but to the pleasant plucking of guitar strings that he was familiar with.

Eventually, he caught on to a gentle melody that was ever so familiar to him. He let the soothing tune guide him, and at last, there she was, at the end of the street, performing on a small portable stage. A smile spread across his lips, and he quickened his pace, eager to see her and hear the remainder of the story she was telling.

She was telling a captivating tale about Kath, an enthusiastic explorer in search of a fountain of youth, and the hefty price she paid upon its discovery, as well as the numerous hardships she encountered on her journey towards it.

When he approached, winded from his brisk pace, and in that moment, the bard's melody distorted. It shifted from a beautiful, charming tune that captivates all listeners into an agonizing plucking of out-of-tune strings. It lacked rhythm and harmony. Her face began to morph, turning from a gorgeous, alluring woman with long snow-white hair, into an elderly woman with missing hair and a disfigured face.

He gasped, astonished, his mouth agape with shock as he watched his beloved bard turn from a woman of dreams into a nightmarish hag. The crowd, startled by the sudden transformation of her voice, instrument and body, quickly dispersed.

"**NOOOA!!!**" she howled. Her gaze fell upon the rogue; "What have you **DONE**?"

His feelings for her faded as soon as her face changed, but it was more than just the looks - it was something else. Caden felt as if a string had snapped, as if a charm had been broken. *'A charm?'* he thought to himself, *'This beast charmed me?'*

She threw her guitar at him, an easy dodge for a professional rogue.

"What did you **DO**?"

He reached for his dagger, his love and affection for her were now replaced by anger and frustration. "No! What did **you** do to **me**, you *hag*?"

She let out a howling, bone-chilling scream, much like a banshee.

"I was living the dream! Fame, fortune and fools to give me all that I desired! A **PERFECT** life now lies in ruins because of **YOU**!" she shouted. "You and that cursed anti-magic flower! **BE GONE!**"

She squatted down and darkness enveloped her, wings of shadows sprouted from her back and she leaped into the air. Before Caden had a chance to do anything, a bone-chilling screech echoed through the city's streets, fading by the second as the monster distanced herself, flying away.

"BANSHEE!" A guard standing on the roof of a building called out. His attention shifted from the fleeting demon to the rogue on the street beneath.

"Get the damned antimag flower out of here, you idiot! We can't pursue the demon without magic!"

In silence, Caden turned to leave, to run, to flee with his conflicted feelings. He darted down the cobblestone street. Occasionally, an object or a person would crash or fall in his vicinity. That was until he himself tumbled down onto the stoney street after running into someone. A flash of purple momentarily filled his vision.

As he scrambled back up to his feet he grunted apologetically, "Ugh! Crap, my bad. I'm in a bit of a hu..." he paused mid-sentence when he noticed Clare laying on the ground in front of him.

The archivist from the library sat up and let out an annoyed sigh.

"I know I'm short. That doesn't mean I'm unnoticeable! Sheesh... I was just looking for you too, and... my phase shift didn't activate?" She examined her hands, there was a small cut on her left palm that she could not heal with a spell.

"Right, anyway, **you** are coming with **me!**" she said and then glanced up. Her eyes widened, and a slight blush painted her cheeks a gentle rosy color when she noticed Caden standing there, offering her a hand to help her up. She took his hand, got up and dusted herself off.

"You got the flower, huh?"

"Y... yeah," he uttered.

She smiled at him sarcastically.

"Wonderful! Delightful! IT! CANCELS! MAGIC!"

She attempted to reach out with her hand to demand that he hands the flower over to her, only to realize she was still holding onto his hand. She swiftly pulled her hand away, breaking the handhold, and then extended it outward, palm up.

"Hand it over."

He reached for the flower in his bag, took it out and carefully placed it in the palm of her hand, still wrapped in cloth.

"Yes... I uhh, noticed that, and got yelled at because of it."

"Rightfully so!"

She carefully unwrapped the legendary, magic neutralizing Meniva flower, and admired it for a moment. Its petals were golden and sparkling, vaguely resembling wheat, but metallic. Its glowing aura was mesmerizing. She wrapped it back up and smiled at the rogue.

"Come with me. You are the first person to find one of these in the past two centuries, I need to document everything for the archives."

He obeyed her demands and followed in her step.

They used a back entrance to the library due to the anti-magic properties of the flower, which had a radius of about five meters, as they had confirmed during their walk. Their primary goal was to ensure that the flower would not interfere with anything or anyone. Especially, they wanted to avoid putting any lives at risk, which would be more than likely at the Grand Library, given the number of wizards that traversed the library in the most unordinary ways.

Once they made it to the archives, the flower was handed over to a couple of grand wizards who sealed it in the library's treasury, a vault — housing magical artifacts of indescribable powers.

His journey for the flower was thoroughly recorded by Clare. She marveled at his encounter with the supreme being, the Overseer. She explained that it was a supreme deity that watched over an inconceivable number of worlds. It was extremely interesting to her, since very few get the opportunity to interact with the Overseer.

"And on that... I believe all the matters have been addressed," she said, closing the tome she was writing in, the very same tome she had learned about the flower from. The tome that was missing half a page before, now had a few brand-new and empty pages in it, upon which she took her notes. Simultaneously, a magic quill transcribed his encounter with the Overseer in a different book, a book he was not allowed to even peek into, let alone touch.

Caden got up to leave. "Well then! I best be on m..." He turned and froze in his tracks when he felt a firm grasp on his shoulder.

"Not so fast, little rogue," Clare spoke in a sly tone. She leaned closer to him. He felt her breath on his ear, and then heard her sweet gentle whisper, that sent shivers through his body.

"I know you have something that doesn't belong to you."

He shivered, "Uhh... s... sorry!" he murmured, admitting his guilt. Slowly, he pulled the *Cooking Rocks with Actual Rocks* out from his pouch, turned around and offered it to her.

She glanced at the book, and then chuckled.

"Oh, these are greeaaaat! The cooking series is by the greatest wizard-chef to have ever existed. He created these magical tomes that can utilize anything for cooking to produce actual, edible meals, out of anything! They're enchanted books. Truly fascinating. Oh, my goodness, he also has one for *'Cooking Insects,'* and..." she continued to ramble about the *Cooking X with X* series for the next half hour. Caden found it amusing, and her company enjoyable.

He did not notice the time passing in her company. She was charming and quirky, and kept telling him about various magic tomes in the archives, even showing some of them to him. When the time came to depart, his farewell was met with a simple question that would change his entire life.

"Say, why don't you come and work for the library? We could use a skilled rogue in the role of an Artifact Scavenger. Honest work, plenty of thrill... right up your alley, no?" Clare asked.

He glanced at the archivist over his shoulder. "I'll... think about it."

And he thought about it. Over the next few days, he found a more permanent dwelling in Rivera and began to frequent the archives, to learn more about the library and how it operates, and to learn more about the quirky and likable archivist he found himself growing fond of rather quickly. However, his desire to hunt down the banshee and take revenge still remained, though that desire faded away over time, and got replaced by his new duties that kept him busier than ever before. He became more and more content with his new life, new responsibilities, and his newfound and true love.

And so begins a new chapter of his tale, but not in this book.

Snow Rose

At the break of dawn, behind the frosted window that twinkled in the rays of early morning sun, stood a young girl. She sipped on a steaming hot beverage out of a wooden mug. Her warm breath thawed the thin layer of frost on the window before her. The white forest outside her window was painted in orange hues. Rays of sunlight made the snow glisten playfully for her eyes, and only hers. It was a little morning spectacle for her. Upon finishing her drink and setting the wooden mug down, she got dressed in warm fur clothes she had previously obtained from a local merchant who dropped by weekly. She also gathered some basic tools that she always carried with her during her outings: a small ice pick and a shovel.

Before opening the door, which separated her comfort and warmth from the winter's cold which would soon be pinching her cheeks, she paused to examine the list of ingredients she had to gather to complete her order:

Crystal icicle
Frost shrooms
Eggs of the winter dwelling essin
Molted skin of the snow spiders

The list was finished off with a few simpler and more basic ingredients, listed at the bottom.

The bark of a pine tree
A handful of fresh pine needles
Dried oak leaves
Bark of a birch tree

She read the list attentively, memorizing each ingredient. "Medicinal potions yet again? Alrighty," she remarked to herself in a playful tone, then took a deep breath of the comfortably warm air before swinging the door into the harsh coldness open. *Harsh as the environment may have seemed, she found peace in this forest, away from people, and in quiet solitude. This was her home.*

The gentle crunching of snow beneath her thick winter boots brought serenity to her ever-wandering thoughts. The twinkling snow in the morning sun put a smile on her face, and although the frost pinched her cheeks, the crisp air that filled her lungs with every breath brought a sense of clarity to her mind and body alike.

The journey was rather uneventful. On her way, she stumbled upon several of Essin's nests, gathering a handful of eggs from them. Frost shrooms were also available in abundance in this part of the forest - finding and collecting them did not pose a challenge to someone well acquainted with the Frosted Forest, and the same applied to most other ingredients on her list.

She moved through the snowy landscape with the surprising ease and elegance of an elk. Each step she took was firm and confident, yet knowledgeable. She skillfully avoided branches and roots hidden beneath the snow that could have posed a tripping hazard and swiftly made her way to the entrance to the caves. Upon knocking the snow off her shoes by the entrance, she began her search for the nests of snow spiders, and to her surprise, she found none by the entrance.

"Odd," she remarked. It was as if something drove them deeper into the caves. It was no colder than usual, and there were no natural predators for them, not here at least.

She pulled out a crystal from her pouch and drew a rune of some kind on the floor of the cave. Upon completion, she removed her mitten and placed the bare palm of her hand on the freezing-cold stone. Closing her eyes, she calmed her breathing.

'Slow and steady. In and out.'

She searched for abnormalities in the magic winds. Something caught her attention momentarily, but it was shallow, insignificant. She dismissed it, nothing else seemed too out of the ordinary to raise suspicion. With a relieved sigh, she completed her investigative ritual and then headed into the cave. She encompassed her necklace with her hands and whispered something to it in a language that was different from her native tongue. It was a pendant depicting a boy holding out a heart-shaped lantern. The heart-shaped lantern began to glow brightly, illuminating the area around her as a full-sized lantern would.

Previously she had never ventured beyond the second fork, and as such she only memorized the cave system up to that point. However, despite her persistent search, not a single snow-spider nest was to be found.

"Even deeper?" She eyed the splitting cavern passage before her, standing at the second fork. The path forward was dark, yet invitingly warm. The further she went, the warmer it got. It was comforting to the point that she even contemplated making this cave system her dwelling, but she dismissed that thought once more, *'no no, Cave Witch just sounds far too sinister,*' she reminded herself. That would indeed have been an inferior title compared to her current one: *The Witch of the Permafrost.*

She marked the route she took with a crystal by drawing on the stone wall with it, leaving behind a glowing rune. Taking a deep breath, she mustered up her courage. *'Relax Mitra. It'll be fine. Deep breaths, just like Professor Ulter taught you,'* she thought to herself, still holding her breath in.

'Breathe out, you fool!' She reminded herself.

After a few brief moments of breathing exercises, she steadied her rapidly beating heart and headed further into the oddly welcoming darkness. Each step she took echoed through the otherwise silent cave, informing all — of her presence.

Her search for the snow-spider nests lasted a couple of hours. Although she had not been past the second fork before, nothing much changed after it. The cave remained much the same - mostly empty - occupied by a few varying species of insects and some other small creatures, arachnids, and critters.

At last, she rejoiced when she stumbled upon dozens of the snow-spider nests and proceeded to collect the rarest ingredient she currently required: their molted skins, gathering twice as many as she needed to avoid having to venture so deep into the cave again, in the near future. The skins neither spoil nor lose their effectiveness, so a more resourceful approach seemed better to her in this case.

After gathering all she required, she exited the cave. A quick glance revealed that the sun was still high in the sky. It appeared to be late in the afternoon, but still a long while till dawn. Mitra estimated that the trip back would take approximately an hour, and a few more to brew the potions and prepare the order. Concluding that she did not have the time for sightseeing on the way back, she examined the contents of her pouch and verified that she had indeed gathered all of the necessary ingredients to fulfill her outstanding orders for various potions. On that note, she decided to return to her hut and get working on fulfilling the order.

After a while of walking through the mundane whiteness, off in the distance, Mitra spotted a herd of deer traveling through the forest. She watched them closely: A full herd, well over fifty of them, were moving steadily through the snowy forest. *'Odd... deer don't usually venture this far into the forest during the winter.'* She made a mental note and attentively scanned the area around her. Other than the seemingly migrating herd of deer, the forest was eerily quiet and lifeless. While the Frosted Forest was not the liveliest of regions on the continent around this time of the year, the birds, certain insects, foxes, and small critters still dwelled within these permafrost regions. Yet today, it was the quietest she had seen in ages. Something chased the spiders to move deeper into the caves. Something pushed the deer to migrate through these deep-frozen regions. Something made most creatures hide, yet nothing seemed abnormal to her.

She diverted her course, taking a detour and putting distance between herself and the herd so as not to spook and stress them out when they seemed so cautious already. Her mind raced with possibilities, listing, and dismissing each after another, as she carefully threaded the deep snow.

'Hunters? No, they never come to the Northern side, and wouldn't venture near a witch's dwelling. An apex predator making its way through the forest? I don't sense bloodlust though,

lest it's merely passing through... no, that wouldn't have caused a whole herd to move, and spiders in the caves hardly care for predators. A new wizard? Or a witch in the area? Hardly possible, I'd have noticed the intruder's energy. Perhaps a natural disaster is imminent? Albeit unlikely, as birds would have informed me.'

Unable to pinpoint the potential cause of the odd behavior of the forest, Mitra chose to dismiss these concerns until tomorrow. Tonight's orders took priority and with no direct and imminent threat facing her, she had no reason not to fulfill the request.

As she neared her dwelling, her hut came into view off in the distance, enshrouded by the barren tree trunks. It was another half a kilometer away, maybe less. Her lips curled up into a gentle smile, but the smile washed away just as suddenly a moment later. Her focus was drawn to a strange glisten in the snow by a tree, a few dozen meters ahead of her.

'Odd, what is that?' Suddenly, a silly thought sprung up in her mind, *'Snow Rose?'* And then the eerie silence of the forest was broken by her own snarky giggle.

"Haha! What are you saying, you silly girl? Snow rose? The rarest of flowers, blossoming right in your path? What are the chances?"

She ridiculed herself for even having that thought.

The snow continued to crunch and squeak under her boots as she slowly made her way toward the glistening object. It was no easy feat to frighten a witch, especially in her domain. Although she was neither a witch of snow nor ice, she had made this forest her dwelling, and as such, it would take a great deal of effort to make her uneasy.

She neared the tree and her jaw dropped when she could finally see the glistening object that rested under the tree. Only half of it was illuminated by the sun. Mitra could not believe what she was seeing before her. "S... snow rose?" She stuttered, taking a calculated and slow step closer, approaching the plant to confirm her suspicion.

From beneath the cotton-white snow protruded a crystalline stem, atop of which was a rose bulb, aqua-blue in color and transparent, as if made of perfectly clear ice. Its leaves resembled paper-thin sheets of diamonds. A single leaf peeked from the shadow cast upon it by the mighty oak, standing guard over the delicate artifact. The leaf was the sole one to be hit by a ray of light, refracting the sun's blessing into a colorful iridescence, projecting a whole rainbow upon the snow beneath it.

She knelt beside the rose, admiring its beauty. Her mind raced in disbelief as she quickly combed her memories for scarce bits of useful information about these incredibly rare flowers.

'There are only ever a handful of them blossoming worldwide at any given time. They sell for an astronomical price since the aristocrats love gifting rare things to their daughters, and these flowers are also said to bring good luck. Extremely delicate yet resilient to all the weather and natural conditions and elements. Once it blossoms, it will never wither and the snow, from which it grows, will never melt, lest the flower is broken, but it too, will never melt.'

Mitra removed her mittens and traced the paper-thin leaf of the plant. Her hands trembled, but she focused on keeping the finger steady. It was ice-cold, as one would expect of a flower named Snow Rose.

She smiled, sat her bag down, and steadily removed the shovel and icepick from her belt, essential tools she always carried with her. She began by tracing out a circle with her bare hands in the snow around the plant, creating a groove to follow with her shovel. Then, with a shovel, she carefully dug the depth of snow around the created perimeter.

The roots seemed to run roughly ten centimeters deep, and she dug to that depth. Mitra emptied her bag, and then carefully dug out the plant the rest of the way. She slid the bag under the groove she dug out and finished off the job, the plant was now firmly secured in her bag. As she lifted the bag, and brought it forth into the sun, the rose glistened even brighter and more magnificently than before. Its leaves projected rainbows all around onto the snow beneath. The flower bulb itself sparkled, resembling a starry night sky on a clear, moonless night. The flower was like a perfectly carved sculpture frozen in time. She found herself absolutely mesmerized by this incredible plant.

Having only ever read the briefest mentions of it in books at the academy, she never even dreamed of seeing it in person.

Mitra left behind the ingredients she had collected at the site where she had found the flower, as her only desire currently was to safely bring the rose back to her hut. Upon reaching it, she burst through her door. The warm air tickled her cheeks and irritated her throat and lungs which were used to the chilly outside air. She coughed lightly while making her way to the kitchen where she carefully sat the plant down on the windowsill, next to a wooden cup with a now cold, herbal brew.

Mitra had to force herself to peel away from the mesmerizing plant that kept mesmerizing her, to head back out and recollect the ingredients she previously had to toss out of her bag. It was a quick trip back and just as quick of a return. She carefully planted the Snow Rose in a clay pot and then sat back on the windowsill. Her work of potion brewing began. She steadily prepared each potion and crossed them off her order list, hours passed in a blink. Each brew was carefully poured into a one-liter bottle and capped off thereafter, ready for the merchant to pick them up. She hardly had the time to begin brewing herself a relaxing drink and jotting down the details of the day in her diary, when a knock on the door distracted her.

"Come in!" she called out, keeping her focus on the diary, attempting to hastily finish her notes.

The door creaked open and through it stepped a snow-covered, mildly chubby, middle-aged man, sporting a fabulous mustache, and reddish cheeks that had been pinched by the frost outside.

"My, my, Mitra, dearie! How do you survive in this wilderness and cold?" He took his mittens and hat off, rubbing his hands in a desperate attempt to warm them up.

She shrugged casually. "I wonder... guess I enjoy weather that is as cold as my heart. One moment please," she replied half dreamily while noting down the list of abnormalities she had encountered in the forest today and finishing it off with the mention of discovering the ever so rare and mesmerizing flower, the Snow Rose.

He nodded, patiently waiting for her to wrap up whatever it was she was busy with. A fire pit at the center of her dining room warmed her hut, giving off a welcoming and homely feel to the cold visitor.

His gaze was fixated on the fire pit, above which a small kettle hung. The liquid within was just starting to boil. A faint whistle informed Mitra that the brew was ready.

"Right on time!" she said, closing her diary and leaving it on the kitchen counter. She grabbed a wooden cup and poured it half full of the herbal brew.

"How do you fare today, Mister Sterl?" she inquired, offering him the cup with steaming liquid.

He accepted the drink with no hesitation, grasping the cup with his cold fingers in search of comforting warmth.

"Ohh quite well. Thank you, dearie!" A whiff of pleasant, minty aroma from the cup instantly soothed his busy mind. He took a sip. The pleasant warmth traveled down his throat, carrying the refreshing coolness of mint along with a hint of bitterness and a lingering, flowery aftertaste.

"Gahh! Just perfect dearie. Your tea never fails to surprise me," he remarked as his curious gaze wandered around the interior of the rather small, wooden hut.

"And yourself? How are you faring in this wilderness?"

Mitra smirked, took a sip of the brew, and followed his curious gaze.

"It is not much, but it is mine. Not much changes around here, but I've grown rather fond of this dwelling - no small part, thanks to you Mister Sterl." She bowed her head down respectfully to the merchant who had been nothing but a pleasure to work with.

He has always been kind, and eager to trade her potions for anything she would request, along with home delivery of desired goods.

He glanced at the young witch.

"Oh no, no! Please don't mention it. Your *kind* is... rather rare. How could I not go above and beyond to accommodate you, who ever-so-generously takes care of our town?"

She raised her head back up and smiled. "Whatever do you mean? There are other witches besides me in this region."

He nodded. "C... certainly, but none are quite so easy to work and make deals with as you are."

He seemed nervous for the briefest of moments. After taking another sip, his nervousness dissipated and was replaced by a pleased sigh.

"Ahhh! That truly hits the spot... Ah, right! I brought the desired kitchenware, and I had the leather crafter make you the finest backpack per your request - all's in my cart!" He confirmed his part of the bargain. "Did I forget anything?"

"No, don't think so. I have the new list of wares prepared. It's hanging on the door. And the potion order has been completed as agreed - the bottles are crated and are awaiting by the door."

The merchant glanced over his shoulder at the door. At first, he focused on the list that was pinned to the wall: It was too far away to read, but it appeared to be rather short. His gaze then drifted to the side, where, by the door, against the wall - two wooden crates stood, filled with bottles. He smiled, pleased.

"You're just a delight, dearie."

She smiled shyly, "Oh please, I'm sure others aren't quite so bad to deal with as you make it sound."

He let out an annoyed humph, "You went to the academy, you've seen them firsthand!"

Mitra let out a snort. "True, many are rather stuck-up." Suddenly she gasped when the sound of the wooden cup impacting the floor echoed through the cabin.

"Are you alright?"

The merchant lifted his trembling hand, pointing a shaking finger at the rose that decorated the windowsill, shimmering beautifully in rays of the setting sun that was beaming through the frosted glass.

"Is... is that? Th... that can't be!" He stuttered through words in a desperate attempt to speak, despite the great shock.

Mitra almost spat her drink out from the humorous sight of the merchant. His expression and even posture resembled a *raccoon who got caught stealing food in the dead of night.* She suppressed her desire to chuckle and slowly turned to follow his pointing finger. Her lips curled up into a smirk, but the awestruck merchant remained frozen in place, like a stalactite. She slowly got up, walked around the table, picked up the wooden cup, and then sat it back on the table.

"Mister Sterl? Are you alright?"

He slowly peeled his gaze from the mesmerizing plant he could not believe to be sitting on her windowsill and then stared in awe at Mitra.

"D... do you not... is... is that?" he stuttered in disbelief; the sight of the rare artifact rendered him, a renowned merchant, speechless.

She smiled at him warmly. "I believe so, Snow Rose, yes."

To her surprise, his jaw dropped even lower as he returned his focus to the legendary flower. "M... may I?"

"Sure, but it's rather fragile, please do not touch it."

"C... certainly dear!" He practically ran up to the flower, admiring it from a closer distance, without touching it.

"It is everything I ever thought it would be! Magnificent! Grandiose! No! It is far more than everything... I... I have no words," he kept stumbling over his own words and then paused.

"Pay! I'll... I'll p-pay anything for it," he spoke without tearing his gaze from the flower.

Mitra shook her head, tossed a rag over the spilled liquid on her floor, and then approached him from behind. Each step she took was light and calculated.

"Not sure I want to sell it, not yet at least."

The merchant turned around; his expression shifted from awestruck to pleading.

"Anything Mitra. ANYTHING AT ALL!" He offered confidently.

"Mmhhgg..." she groaned with a hint of annoyance. "Not now!" Her voice was stern and focused. Her gaze darted to the crates by the wall. "Will that be all?"

The merchant followed her glance and then recollected his composure.

"Ah... but of course, dearie! However, should you change your mind, my offer shall remain on the table." He articulated with his hands like a maestro, clearly eager to get his hands on this rarity.

A thought flashed through Mitra's mind, *'Need to refresh the defensive seals.'* A silly thought she did not think she would ever have when dealing with Mister Sterl. He was a reputable and honest merchant, but his eagerness was far more than she had anticipated.

"Of course, Mister Sterl." She gave him a weak smile. "I wouldn't even consider offering it to anybody else, should the desire to trade it ever arise."

A sliver of doubt crept up and mixed into his pleading expression, as he examined her confident face carefully. His eyes darted between hers and for a moment, his heartbeat drowned out everything. *Thump*. Was there anything she was hiding? *Thump*. Nothing as far as he could tell; she just seemed tired. *'Poor thing...' Thump. 'Was she...'*

Suddenly he became aware of her questioning look and realized that he had been staring. He took a deep breath and lowered his gaze. And with that, the time returned to normal. The quietness and the tension he felt were replaced by the sound of the surroundings, flooding back into his head once more. It was as if someone had suddenly unmuted the world around him. He let out a resigning sigh.

"Right! Excellent! What a find though, color me impressed. Not only are you an incredible potion maker, but also unbelievably lucky."

She shrugged. "I just wish to help, despite," she paused for a moment, "The limitations that I face."

The merchant's demeanor shifted from excitement to concern. "The... hemophobia, yes? Poor lass."

She offered a weak smile. "Maybe magic isn't my forte, but my knowledge is still valuable."

He nodded. "Right. I'll bring the goods right away." Taking the crates with him, he left.

A few brief moments later he returned with a sack over his shoulder and a crate under his left arm. He gently sat both on the floor.

"Fresh produce and the wares you requested."

"Much obliged."

He bowed slightly toward her. "Always a pleasure, dearie. And, if you do decide to sell that rose, I assure you, I'll accept **any** price you would desire for it, the king himself would purchase it off of you."

She gave him a weak smile and nodded. "I will keep that in mind. A cup of tea before you head back?"

The merchant glanced out the frosted window and took a deep break, "Oh no, no, much as I appreciate the lovely offer, I best be on my way to avert traveling in the dark."

She nodded. "Safe travels, Mister Sterl."

"A good and restful night to you, dearie."

And just like that, the merchant found himself traveling back through the Frosted Forest on a horse-drawn wagon. The setting sun painted the whiteness in orange hues, giving the forest a surreal vibe - a lovely scenery that he grew fond of after dozens of trips. However, even this beautiful scenery could not erase the vivid image of the magnificent Snow Rose that had embedded itself in his mind. Just as he found himself powerless to the allure of the flower, so did Mitra. She watched the beautiful, ice-sculpture-looking plant glisten for her in the setting sun for a while, before at last she succumbed to her exhaustion.

A couple of hours past midnight, she awoke from an unfamiliar screech. Her eyes opened slowly, without haste, and she blinked sleepily in an attempt to bring her disoriented vision to focus. A few blinks later she realized that the shadow that stood on the table before her was not natural. Slowly peeling her head from the table, she leaned back, observing the creature before her. In the moonlight, on either side of the clay pot in which the Snow Rose was planted, stood two shades, or rather — black, fuzzy-looking, shadow-like shapes, each with four legs. Mitra observed the shapes, they remained motionless, at first. When she leaned closer to take a better look, the creatures leaned back, as if attempting to keep distance.

Her mind raced through possibilities: *'Shadow fiends - non hostile, low rank spirits that like to play pranks, harmless but a nuisance. No, can't be them, shadow fiends are flying spirits and have no defined shape, unlike these two fellas. Perhaps a forest-dweller? No, they're larger, at least the size of a kitten.'*

She crossed off the most obvious possibilities one after another in her mind. Sizing the creatures up, she slowly brought a finger closer to one of them to grasp the size and their reactions better. They were small... quite small in fact, no larger than a mouse. Strange and fuzzy. They looked hairy but distorted as if shadows manifested and took up shape and volume. This indicated they were either fey or spirits, perhaps elementals, all of which - it should be noted - are vastly different from one another in shape, behavior, and intentions.

The anatomy of these creatures was strange as well, more akin to spirits in the sense that they were a single blob of existence. The legs protruded from the fuzzy ball-shaped bodies that also served as their heads as it would seem. At random the creatures sprouted a semblance of an eye anywhere on their body. When her finger got closer, the creature nearest to the finger leaned back on its four legs, and the semblance of the eye, which previously was at the front, would move to the back, away from potential harm.

Occasionally, the creatures would glance at each other, and then their *eyes* would disappear, or shift back to the front to stare at Mitra. No matter how hard Mitra thought about it, these creatures did not fit into any category she was aware of. She carefully placed her hand on the table, palm down, and then lifted her index finger, pointing at the creature on the left side, closest to her.

It watched her hand intently, then sprouted another eye that kept a close watch on her eyes. A moment later, the creature that was closest to her, took a few tiny steps forward. Extending one of its legs, as if cautiously reaching for her finger. Mitra watched the fuzzy creature as it cautiously, yet with equal curiosity, approached her. The creature's leg continued to grow longer and longer until it stopped a centimeter away from her finger. It hesitated and then pulled its leg back. Mitra chortled playfully at the shy creature.

"Dawhh, it's alright. I won't harm you."

The creatures froze in place. Their eyes moved to stare at each other and then in unison, their bodies shook. A high-pitched and childish-sounding giggle echoed out of their bodies.

Mitra gasped, taken aback by the sudden imitation of the chortle. Once more her mind rushed through a list of possible magical creatures. There were not many creatures in existence that imitated humans, or other living beings, and those that did, usually did so - not with good intentions. *Leshy? Kind of fits... a forest spirit that imitates sounds and can create illusions.*

They're defenders, guardians of forests, highly intelligent, but shy, and generally avoid humans and witches.'

Their giggle soon ended, and in awkward silence she stared at the creatures that stared back, blinking at her, or pretending to at least.

"Do... you understand me?"

Their reaction was pretty identical to the one before: They sprouted another eye to glance at each other while keeping the spare eye firmly focused on the young witch before them. A moment later their bodies buzzed as they replied in unison in the same, high-pitched childish voice she had just heard.

"Yes, we do!"

Mitra gasped. She swiftly pulled her hand back, surprised and startled by a response rather than an imitation.

"What... are you? Leshy?"

The creatures seemingly blinked, and as their eyes closed, they never reopened, they disappeared. All except the one that was focused on Mitra. Their childish voices reverberated in unison once more.

"We are Urtid. I am Urtid. We seek home, home with witch! We desire to serve. We crave to help." Their words, its words, did not particularly instill confidence or trust in her, yet she felt no threat in their speech.

"Wait! Hold on... backtrack a little. *We are? I am?* Please elaborate."

The creature closest to her took a step back, while the one further away slithered into the shadow and popped out next to the first. The two fuzzy shadow spider-like creatures, the Urtid, as they introduced themselves, performed a gesture that Mitra could only interpret as a *courteous bow.* The creatures spoke again. Its voice morphed to a more normal and adult-sounding voice, far more pleasant to the ear and perfectly pitched, neither male nor female, a voice that could be either.

"Urtid is a mind. A collecting mind, a symphony of all. We are Urtid, creatures of Urtid. Connected and living, thinking as one. A colony of Urtid is but one Urtid in mind."

Mitra raised her eyebrows, lost in thoughts.

'Hive mind colony creature by the name of Urtid... does not ring any bells.'

"I see, a hive mind! Akin to a colony of bees, working and living together for the benefit of the colony. But you're not an organic creature, you're magical, no doubt. So how come I've never heard of you at the academy?" She reached for her necklace and grasped it tightly with her left hand as if expecting the answers to her questions from it. The chilly sensation of the cold metal helped her focus and brought a sense of serenity to her mind.

"Not for colony. Urtid exists to find a home. To serve, to aid, to guide, a witch... we exist for only a short while. When a witch of blood, darkness, or nature, finds a snow rose, then and only then do we, Urtid, spawn to serve the witch or witcher. We exist for exactly seven days. Once the time is up, at midnight of the seventh day, all memories of us perish, along with our existence."

Mitra tilted her head to the side. "Your..." but before she could ask any follow-up questions, the creatures vigorously shook their bodies, like two wet dogs shaking out their wet fur, and then continued.

"Mighty witch, the blood witch, we Urtid shall serve and teach you." They raised their hind legs, pointing at the rose.

"The witch of blood can activate the power of the rose to bring back the dead." Spoke the creature on the right.

"The witch of shadow can summon a high rank demon servant that shall obey," continued the creature on the left. "And the witch of nature can make the flower wither in an instant, leaving behind seeds of life that can revive a dying forest," spoke a voice from the ceiling, the same voice as before, a unisex voice, but the direction from which it came startled Mitra a little.

She glanced up at the ceiling to see a dozen or so more of those fuzzy shadow-spider-looking creatures. More and more Urtid poured into her hut from every nook and cranny. As if every shadow and every corner had an Urtid hidden within it. The creatures all buzzed, and in perfectly harmonious unison they spoke: "We will serve the great witch of blood, the chosen witch, the mighty witch, we shall serve you in all your deeds until our time is up."

Mitra lifted her foot as another Urtid crawled past her leg. And then all of them bowed to her simultaneously.

"Aha... so..." she hesitated; her gaze curiously wandered the dozens upon dozens of mysterious creatures that just pledged loyalty to her, for the next seven days.

"So... what *can* you do?"

The original two sprouted another set of eyes to glance at each other.

"Anything," one spoke.

"Whatever you desire," continued the other.

They all spoke in unison. "Anything you wish for, chosen witch, the witch of blood. There are no limits! None exist! Not for us. Not for me. And no longer for you."

Mitra raised her eyebrow, listening attentively to the creatures. "Annnything?" She let out a chuckle. "So, like, taking over the country?"

The creatures remained silent for a moment. "Is such your wish, oh witch of blood?"

"No! No no no no! God no! That was a joke! A JOKE!" she replied in a panicked tone, "Please do **not** conquer anything in my name," she pleaded.

The voice of the creatures morphed into the childish one, and in unison, they giggled once more.

She shuddered. "Uhh, please uhm... speak to me from just one body? It's rather creepy hearing fifty of your voices speaking all at once, or... bouncing between the bodies. Please?"

One of the two original creatures stepped up and spread his two front legs in a sort of *welcome* gesture, like a showman. "As you wish, oh great witch. Our apologies."

Mitra chortled once more. "Oh please, drop the *great,* I'm..." she hesitated, her voice trailed off into a murmur, "hardly great... rather useless, if anything."

"Pardon me?"

Her dreamy gaze traveled from the fuzzy shadow creature before her up to the mesmerizing, crystalline-looking flower bulb in the pot that glistened playfully in the moon's light. A soft sigh escaped her lips. "I'm... any wish huh?"

"Anything you desire, oh chosen witch, within the possibilities of the physical realm, of course."

She pondered for a while. "At the academy, they spoke of an ancient toad that supposedly knows all the secrets to every phobia. Find it, that toad. I wish to know the cure to my phobia!"

"Is such your wish? Oh, great witch."

She nodded firmly. "Yes."

It took but a mere second for all the Urtid creatures to scatter and disappear, except for the one that she had been communing with, one of the original two. Mitra watched in awe as many of them seemingly dissolved into shapeless shadows and slithered through cracks in the walls and floor.

"And...? Wh... what now?"

"Now you wait until we grant your wish."

"That's it? I make a wish, and you go and grant it? No... payment? No catches?"

The single creature before her shook its entire body side to side.

"Most of me will search for that toad. Shall there be not enough of me, more will appear to serve. Until the majority returns with the toad, I and others will serve you here, and fulfill you any other wishes and desires."

Mitra lit the fire and hung the kettle onto the hook above it. Sitting on the stool beside the fire, she seized the opportunity to ask everything she could think of.

"The spider's disappearance in the cave... Is that your doing?"

Urtid shook its body side to side once more, sitting on her knee.

"No. The blossoming of the Snow Rose brings with it disturbances to nature and nature's balance. While the magic aura of the plant is all but inexistent, it is enough for animals to sense the abnormality and act out of normal behavior."

"If I note my memories about you and all of this in my diary, will the records remain?"

"We are a being of mythical nature, only a few had ever met us. All records of our existence will cease to exist with us."

Mitra nodded slowly.

"I see... and, you said previously that only three witch types can unveil the true power of the Snow Rose?"

"Correct. Only a shadow, nature, or a blood witch, such as yourself, will ever unveil the true power of the godly flower. And we, the Urtid, come to existence when such witches or witchers discover the godly flower - the Snow Rose."

"And what about activating the Snow Rose as a blood witch?"

"A single drop of the blood witch's blood is infused with power far beyond imaginable. Her blood holds the power to control life and death. A single drop onto the snow rose will release the true power of the blood. Break off the flower and place it upon a corpse, and when the rose melts, it will bring back the dead from the realm far beyond. The water left behind by the rose will serve as a pool of life through which the spirit can surface once more. All for the low cost of a single drop of blood," the Urtid replied.

Mitra shuddered at the mere mention of blood. "I... that's... great! I'm, hmmm... not doing that." She placed her hands upon her own shoulders, as if hugging herself. Her body shuddered as she tried not to think of spilling her blood upon the Snow Rose.

Over the next few days, she learned from Urtid that – which the professors at the academy, where she had spent half a decade, were clueless about. She learned of mysteries and artifacts in the world that were far beyond anything she had ever imagined.

In the middle of the fifth night, she was awoken by Urtid's neutral voice.

"Oh great witch, the toad has been discovered, and will be brought here within a day."

The morning after, before Urtid returned, a barrage of bangs on the door made her jump out of her bed.

"Mitra!? Mitra please open up!!!" The distressed voice of Mister Sterl could be heard in between the hurried banging.

She tossed on her robe and pulled the door open; the disheveled merchant fell to his knees before her.

"Mitra! We... we need you!" he pleaded.

Her jaw dropped open at the sight that greeted her sleepy eyes; behind the merchant stood more than a dozen armed royal guards in a straight line from a carriage to her door. Half a dozen of Urtid bodies slithered up her robe and lined her shoulders, observing the guards and the merchant attentively, watching for signs of hostility, ready to defend their mistress. Before she had the chance to utter a single word in response, the carriage's door flung open.

"The king needs you! The nation needs you!"

Her gaze darted down to the pleading merchant on his knees and then back to the carriage. *'Of course, how did I not notice instantly, the royal crest... king? Why?'* She wondered. Too cautious to make a move, she observed. From inside the carriage, the king's concerned gaze met her curious one. A moment later he moved, picked something - or rather, someone - up, and slowly walked down the two steps of the carriage, carrying in his arms his youngest daughter. His face showed no signs of hostility, only concern and worry.

"Mitra please! The princess, she... she's dying!" the merchant spoke, slowly rising to his feet.

"The best medics and healers couldn't help her, and you're the most skillful witch in this region."

She nodded, stepping aside, watching the king as he carefully and steadily took one step after another, approaching her. The guards one after another turned to follow his royal majesty as he passed them.

His golden-hued eyes met Mitra's silvery moons. He lowered his gaze to look at his pale daughter's face and then bowed his head down. A single, soft-spoken word escaped his lips.

"Please."

Mitra took a shaky breath, trying to keep her composure, she offered a welcoming gesture. "Inside, lay her on the bed, it's to the left."

"And the guards?" inquired Mister Sterl.

Mitra sighed. "It's freezing outside, but tell them to be quiet. They may rest by the fireplace." The royal guards nodded affirmatively and poured inside her little hut.

She exampled the sickly princess.

"What happened? Give me everything. Leave out no details."

She traced the princess's body with her fingers, feeling for traces of energy. Simultaneously, Urtid's numerous bodies swarmed the princess.

The king merely shook his head. "I know nothing. She was in good health, and then, as swiftly as the changing winds, she fell gravely ill. It has been three days now, and her condition only deteriorated, despite the best efforts from our finest healers."

Mitra nodded, sensing intertwined paths of energy throughout her body. *A curse. A powerful one, intertwined. Choking out her energy flow. This is a grand wizard difficulty curse... I can't undo it.*

"Save my beloved daughter, and I will pay any price. Half a kingdom or anything else you desire, anything for her!" The king's voice trembled with desperation. When Mitra glanced up at his royal majesty, he was looking down at the floor, overwhelmed by his own powerlessness, shame, and grief. She watched several tears drip from the tip of his nose. A soft sniffle followed.

"I... will try my best."

The king turned around and marched out of the hut. Each step was weak, and heavy with grief.

The rest of the day Mitra tirelessly tended to the dying princess, brewing potions one after another and casting enchantments to slow the spread of the curse that was progressing at an astronomical pace. Although she knew her efforts were in vain, she could not live with herself if she did not at least try her very best.

"Urtid! Can't you do anything about it?"

"Certainly, within limits. We can seek out a grand wizard but not resolve the situation ourselves."

"But you're a magical creature!"

"Mythical," corrected Urthid. "We possess limited magical abilities, not limitless."

"You said you can grant any wish," pleaded Mitra.

"Within possibilities of the physical realm. Request a pyramid to be built in your honor and it shall be done with the aid of a million Urtid, but desire to speak with the deity and it is beyond our abilities. We would seek an artifact, or a person, who could make it happen," the Urtid explained. "Finding and bringing a grand wizard here would take more than a day, I am afraid, it would be a day far too long," they concluded.

"I know..." Mitra replied in a shaky voice. "If only..." she clenched her fist, watching the princess's breathing get heavier by the second.

The clock rang, it was midnight. The princess still fought for her life, and Mitra still tended to the dying royalty on her bed. Urtid's numerous bodies emerged at last through the chimney. The guards were fast asleep by now. Her eyes glistened with hope as she watched the pile of creatures form on the edge of the bed, and then slither away, leaving behind a displeased, old-looking toad in a robe.

The toad glanced around the homely hut, at the gorgeous snow rose that decorated the windowsill, and then at the princess who was struggling to breathe.

"Do you care to explain my abduction?" the toad spoke in an elderly woman's voice.

"Oh, ancient toad, the wise one. Please share your wisdom with me. Help me save the life of an innocent girl who is dying on my bed." Mitra's voice was weak and soft from exhaustion, nearly collapsing from desperately attempting to keep the princess alive throughout the day.

The toad glanced over her shoulder once more. "That she is."

"Share the secret to my phobia with me, the cure! It is said you know them all!" she called out to the frog, falling to her knees before the bed. "It is said you know the secrets of fear, and that you alone can cure any single one, no matter how absurd."

The toad's gaze darted back to the snow rose. "I see. A dying girl. A pleading witch, and a snow rose. Witch of blood are ya, youngling? And what is it that caused you to send that army of those filthy things after me? You need not an old toad to save this girl when you possess the rose."

Mitra pulled herself together. Regaining her composure slightly, she leaned back and sighed heavily. "I have a tremendous fear of blood. The mere sight of a single drop is enough to send me into a stupor. More than a drop would make me faint," she admitted to her weakness and fear before the ancient toad.

The toad listened attentively, and then an elderly woman's snicker echoed through the hut, awakening some of the guards from their slumber.

"Khehehehe, a witch of blood with fear of blood! Oh how ironic. Ah, truly an unfortunate soul you are, young witch." She glanced at Mitra and bowed respectfully. "You have my sincerest sympathy. Very well, I will help you save the child by curing your hemophobia. You'll owe me a favor that I shall not name until the time to call upon it comes. Do you dare accept such a bargain?"

To her surprise, the young witch's resolve was unshaken by such an ominous proposal. "I accept your offer, oh ancient one."

Without a moment's delay, the toad nodded and then leaped up, landing on Mitra's head. She instantly began to chant in ancient Ekser, a language Mitra was vaguely familiar with from her studies at the academy. Chants in this ancient tongue were difficult to control as a single mishap in pronunciation would throw the entire spell off.

After a moment Mitra succumbed to growing tiredness. Her eyes closed, and darkness consumed her.

The following several hours were torturous. In lucid dreams, she was forced to face her worst fears one after another. Reliving them endlessly for what felt like an eternity. Blood elementals caused her blood to boil underneath her skin. Blood demons drained her of blood over and over. Cultists forced her to consume it to undergo the ritual of cleansing.

At some point, she could no longer tell if what she experienced was dreams or reality. She endured the suffering and the tortures, facing each one dozens, and some even hundreds of times over, until at last she persevered and found herself standing in a puddle of blood. It dripped from her fingertips, beneath her feet lay a blood demon, drained of blood and disfigured. *I did this...'* her voice echoed in her mind. *'Such is my power, the power of blood.'* Off in the distance, Mitra caught a glimpse of an eerie scene: a stone ritual altar with a bloodied corpse of a woman atop it, and a cloaked figure carrying away a blood-covered, crying, child.

A gasp escaped Mitra's lips. Dread washed over her as she recognized this scene. She knew that woman and the child.

Memories that had seemingly been sealed, or forgotten, resurfaced at last, giving her insight into her past, and the origin of her phobia. A shiver ran down her spine, anger boiled deep within her. She awoke with a sudden, terrified gasp from the horrendous sight that the toad forced her to witness. Before her, on the edge of the bed, the toad sat with a sly smirk on her face.

"Congratulations, young witch. For you have survived the ancient spell of torment. You faced your worst fears and learned the root cause of your fear. You persevered. A mighty witch you are, and a strong, pure soul," the toad remarked and then let out a cackle. "Hehe, so tell me, my child. What is your greatest fear."

Mitra, still shaken up by the horrors she had just lived through, took a long, slow breath - to steady her heart, and then let it out. Her gaze focused on the toad, cold and stern at first, but slowly her lips curled into a gentle smile.

"I... guess I kind of fear deep waters? You know, when it's so deep it looks like the abyss itself is beneath you?" Mitra's head throbbed but she tried to smile all the same. A sense of fear and uneasiness washed over her. She felt as if a piece of her was now missing. Though, at the same time, she felt like she had regained a piece of her past that had been long forgotten. She closed her eyes; the scene of a bloodied woman's corpse on the stone altar flashed before her once more. She dismissed the vivid image from her mind and concentrated. A few slow breaths helped her regain her concentration. She focused on her blood flow, controlling it. A moment later, the throbbing headache disappeared.

She let out a sigh of relief and reopened her eyes, got up from the floor, and scanned the lifeless body of the princess up and down.

"So still..."

The toad leaped aside and nodded.

"She found her peace at last. Well? What's it going to be, young witch?"

Mitra blinked slowly and turned on her heel, heading toward the rose. The guards that were awake all stepped aside, remaining silent, waiting to observe whatever miracles were about to unfold before them, kicking those that were still asleep to wake them.

She traced the edge of the icy leaf with her finger; the paper-thin leaf cut her fingertip with ease. Lifting her finger over the flower's bulb, she rejoiced as she watched a drop of her own blood fall from her fingertip onto the godly flower beneath.

The flower's leaves grew larger and shifted color to a maroon red, as did the stem. The bulb absorbed her blood instantly, maintaining its transparency and crystal-like appearance while changing its hue from blue to a blood-red tone.

She reached for the stem and snapped it with ease. It shattered with a faint sound that resembled the breaking of an icicle. In her fingers she now carefully held this delicate artifact that could bring back the dead. She carried the sublime flower carefully to the bedside and knelt by it, placing the flower upon the chest of the deceased young princess.

The plant instantly melted into a puddle on her chest. And in that instant, a loud, surprised gasp echoed through the room, followed by numerous sighs of relief from the guards, the toad, and the witch herself.

The princess snapped her eyes open and sprang up into a seated position in an instant, gasping for air as if she had forgotten how to breathe. She scanned the unfamiliar environment, her shock and confusion deepened with everything her gaze fell upon: drying herb racks, a dozen of royal guards scattered around a small wooden hut, Mister Sterl weeping in the corner, a young woman with a beautiful smile kneeling beside the bed, an old toad in a robe watching her from the edge of selfsame, and fuzzy black shadow balls crawling around on the bed and walls. Each thing she looked at seemed more unbelievable than the previous one.

"Where am I?" the princess managed to mutter at last.

"My house," replied Mitra. "You were ill, your father brought you here. Don't worry, rest up." She got up slowly, placed her hand on the princess's head, her skin was warm.

The princess slumped, fell back down and instantly fell asleep again.

"She's alive!" exclaimed one of the guards.

"Praise the..." but he was interrupted by a sudden *Shhh* from Mitra.

"Ler her rest. Inform his majesty of the treatment's success."

What followed later was a lengthy discussion of her wishes that the king swore would be fulfilled: her own clinic in the city, a dwelling near it, and an established trade with herbalists that would deliver all her required ingredients straight to her clinic. With her phobia cured, Mitra finally was able to live out her desired purpose in life: to be a healer and to put her rare gift, blood-magic, to a good cause.

She desired nothing more than to live a peaceful life of helping people with seemingly incurable diseases and health conditions. With time, her fame grew, and her reputation preceded her: *Mitra - the famous blood witch that could cure anything.*

And so her dream came true and people would travel across the oceans in search of her aid. The king's daughter meanwhile regained her energy and grew into a warm-hearted princess, loved by the people and forever grateful for the gift of life that Mitra bestowed upon her.

And thus, the story of Mitra the blood witch – ends. For now...

ANANDA

Panic ensued on the streets.

"Loren, what's going on? The power has gone out." a fretful female voice called out.

Loren released the blinds that he had pried open and threw a glance of discontent over his shoulder. "Pack up, we have to get to the factory," he replied, trying to keep calm.

The woman's eyes widened as she watched Loren read something on his communication device. Provided by his job, it was a small, pager-like device with a screen displaying a scrolling message. He looked up from it anxiously.

"We've got to hurry, the escort is here."

A loud rumble shook the windows of his house and made him jump out of his bed. Cold sweat covered his body, beading on his forehead. After a short while, he finally managed to calm his pounding heart and catch his breath, remaining dazed by how realistic these recurring dreams felt.

A quick glance at the clock revealed that he woke up only ten minutes early, and thankfully would not have to listen to the annoying buzzing of his alarm. After a quick breakfast and a mundane morning routine, Loren was on his way to the lab where he worked. The streets were quiet and mostly empty. Most people commuted by subways, a few brave souls walked to work, and even fewer used bicycles. Occasionally a cyclist would pass him, which was the extent of the traffic he had to deal with. Above-ground transportation was all but obsolete now, and Loren enjoyed the fact that the streets were almost empty - as if exclusive for him alone to use. The walk to work was a peaceful time to clear his mind and think his dreams through. There was no noise and no commotion to distract from his musings.

The buildings lining the empty sidewalks were still mostly dark, as the majority of the population began their workday around noon rather than early in the morning like him.

He kept replaying the events of the dreams in his mind. 'Commotion, panic, and flares. Knocked out power, escort to the factory. Spaceships. An expanding, massive star.' These were the common trends in his dreams. He had seen them all dozens, if not hundreds of times. Sometimes he dreamed of working on a spaceship. Other times he had dreams about the panic and commotion. Sometimes they were dreams about the unknown woman who had seemed so distressed, looking to him for answers as to what was happening. Occasionally he dreamed of a blinding flash of light or explosion. He never seemed to progress past that point though, no matter how hard he tried, the dreams always ended with a blinding flash.

These thoughts kept him busy, making the walk feel shorter than it was. A fifteen-minute walk felt like only a few seconds.

He glanced down at his ID tag hanging loosely on a lanyard around his neck and smiled.

"Still Loren..." he joked, scanning his tag at the door.

The glass wall before him split, opening with a gentle hiss as the card reader turned green. He walked through the large glass door and headed for the elevator. The office was silent, the receptionist greeted him with a sleepy nod before returning her attention to whatever she had at hand. He responded absentmindedly, lost in his thoughts and daydreams.

The elevator arrived with a ding, drawing his focus back to reality. He stepped inside. A few colleagues from different departments greeted him and he responded with a bob of his head and a mumble.

"B - seven, please."

Somebody uttered under their breath, "Time and Space Research, hmm?"

He nodded sleepily.

A few moments of blissful silence came to an end when a smug-faced overweight man in a lab coat tapped Loren on the shoulder. His sarcastic tone was almost painful to listen to.

"Heard you lads at the TSR are getting shut down in a month huh? I would say what a shame, but the true shame is a whole decade with no results."

Loren did not bother as much as glancing over his shoulder; he simply ignored the remark. A younger man next to the one who had spoken let out a chortle, continuing the mockery.

"A whole decade? What a waste of resources. The mag-lev superconductor lab will put their resources to good use."

'This damned elevator couldn't be slower,' Loren thought to himself, trying to ignore the snarky remarks aimed at him and his lab. At long last, the cabin eased to a stop, and an all too familiar ding signaled freedom from the sarcastic remarks. The majority of the people left on this floor, and the next, leaving Loren in the company of a young girl. A teenager by the looks of it, likely a student.

As the elevator hummed back to life and began its gradual descent, he noticed that the girl stood motionless. She did not so much as move a muscle to check the floor at which it stopped. Something was eerie about her, making Loren mildly uncomfortable. Clearing his throat, he tried to spark a conversation.

"Ahem, so, are you a new, uhhmm, intern? Which department?" he inquired curiously in a soft tone, but his questions were ignored. He noticed earbuds in her ears and sighed.

"Right, right, of course. Why did I expect anything else?" he mumbled, watching the lights change until they reached seven under the B column on the left, indicating he had finally reached his lab.

The door slid open and he took his leave. Glancing over his shoulder at the closing doors, he saw the girl still remain perfectly motionless — like a statue, as if frozen in time. She did not blink, or even seemingly breathe. He furrowed his eyebrows, confusion and uneasiness settling in.

'Perhaps she's just lost and confused?' He tried to reason away the oddity he had just witnessed.

As he took a step forward, his attention still glued to the now shut elevator doors, and bumped into the department chief who appeared to be in a rush.

"Oh crap!!! Sorry Chief Shiro! You, uhh, you alright?" Loren scanned the department chief up and down. The chief looked rather worked up and disheveled.

"Ye... yea of course, yeah! All good, uhh, see you later!" he replied, hurrying towards the conference room that was currently in privacy mode.

Loren watched the chief with confusion, then let out a long yawn and made his way to his cubicle. He fired up his workstation and slumped down in his chair. The confusion must have remained on his face, as when his colleague approached him, the question that followed was rather specific as opposed to a mundane How's your morning?

"So, more weird dreams? Bad coffee? Black cat crossed the road? What's up with you?"

Loren jumped slightly at the sound of his colleague's voice, startling him out of his careful concentration of trying to remember his password. "Aaaahhh! Sam!"

"Good job, you remembered my name. What's up with you? You seem, hmm, jumpy."

"That obvious?" he asked while carefully punching his password in on the keyboard, struggling to maintain focus on the task at hand.

"Should see your face…" she replied with a smug grin. Upon glancing at her, he could tell by her expression that he hardly looked composed.

"Well, dreams are a given. Always have those. But today is weird, isn't it? Doesn't something just feel off today?"

Sam scanned the office and then squinted suspiciously.

"Hmmmmmmm, yeah! Now that you mention it. I guess the lights do seem a bit dimmer today huh? How peculiar," she replied, playfully teasing him. "What's up Loren?"

Loren finished inputing his password and entered it with a sigh, turning to face Sam.

"There was this girl in the elevator, a student, but it's like, ugh, she didn't move, you know? I sound insane, but, not even a blink. Kinda creepy. And what's up with Chief Shiro? Why is he so worked up?"

Sam pondered for a moment, listening attentively to what Loren had to say.

"Ah, well the chief thing is easy — we're getting our prototype delivered shortly, so, of course he's all worked up."

Loren's jaw dropped. "Wait, the prototype? Today?"

Sam let out a deep, concerned sigh. "Loren, are you sure you don't need a break? You've been so out of it lately. Yes, the prototype of the time disruptor that we spent a good portion of the past nine years on. And yes, today! In a few hours, in fact."

Loren leaned back in his chair, overwhelmed and feeling dizzy.

"How did I forget something so important?"

Sam leaned a little closer. "Look, Loren, you've been working yourself to the bone lately. After the testing phase is completed, take a vacation, you hear me?"

He nodded, his light blue eyes wide open, finally looking awake, but also concerned.

"Yea yea!" he replied hastily, but it was obvious that his mind was elsewhere and he was no longer paying attention to Sam.

She smiled at him. "Hah... alright, I'll leave you to it. Testing is scheduled for twelve, flat. See you then."

He nodded and turned his attention to work. After a few hours of rushed paperwork and calculations, he printed out and stapled together a set of papers, labeled Time Disruptor Test Sequence. He put them in a folder, and leaned back in his chair to relax his mind a little. His gaze wandered the plain white walls, until his focus was drawn to the clock on the wall. He watched the second hand slowly tick its way around the clock. It read 11:47. 'Funny, in the year of advanced technology and creation of time-disrupting prototypes, we still love a good old cheap mechanical wall clock.'

Each passing second further pushed him into his daydream, and before long he found his consciousness drifting away for a short moment. He jerked back to the waking world and found himself lying on an industrial, metallic grate. The thin metal strips of the catwalk dug into his skin, causing discomfort. A bit of blood painted the gray metal. He pushed himself up with a grunt, wincing from pain that resonated through his body, coming from the wound on his brow. Grabbing onto the railing to support himself, he swiped at his hurting brow, wincing again as his nerves screamed in pain. The noise of heavy machinery and the rush of workers hammering, drilling, and grinding away filled his ears and tore at his disoriented mind, deafening his thoughts.

As he attempted to focus, he noticed a black cat, curled up into a ball by his feet, seemingly having the nap of a lifetime.

He carefully stepped over the cat, pulling a yellow sleeve down to cover his right hand. He pressed it against the wound on his head, soaking up the blood from the small cut on his eyebrow. It was a wound from the fall onto the catwalk from which he had to peel himself. His mind slowly adjusted to the noise of the factory and the dizziness passed. He scanned the environment around him. It was a massive hangar. Rail tracks lined the floor, and two massive engines sat upon train carts, swarmed by workers in a variety of colored jumpsuits. Down on the floor men in purple and blue jumpsuits were discussing things. Heavy machinery roamed freely, carrying materials and parts alike. His head buzzed.

Somehow, the scenery in which he found himself felt familiar but he could not put his finger on it. Then a slow, sleepy meow pulled his drifting mind back into focus. He glanced down at the black cat that had previously been curled and napping. He wondered for a moment if the cat may have been the cause of his fall and the injury. Perhaps it had just decided to keep his body company, assuming he was merely taking a nap. He snorted lightly.

"Heh. Doesn't matter. Come on, kitty cat," he turned and headed for the nearest staircase.

The noise of the factory made it almost impossible for him to focus on his thoughts. At the moment, it did not matter where he was, or how he got there. He just wanted to find some place quiet.

Upon reaching the factory floor, he heard someone call out an all too familiar name.

"LOREN," he paused, glancing around. "LOREN! OVER HERE."

The voice came from his left. From not too far off, a man in a light-blue jumpsuit was jogging toward him. Distress decorated his face.

The man paused to take a deep breath and tried to out-scream the machinery and background noise, "Damn it man! Where you been? The management is going haywire looking for you."

Loren moved his right hand to gesture for the guy to be a little quieter and to slow down. In doing so, he revealed the wound on his head.

"Oh crap!! What happened?" the man in the light-blue jumpsuit exclaimed.

"Ughhh, easy. I'm fine, just slipped."

The other man bobbed his head at the door about a dozen paces from them. As Loren's gaze focused on it, he read the glowing sign above it: Director.

An alarm buzzed and more machinery roared to life. "COME ON! THE EXECS ARE WAITING!" the man in light blue shouted, tugging at Loren's sleeve.

Loren followed, and so did the black cat. Every time Loren gazed over his shoulder to check on his unexpected, furry companion, he would notice the cat's piercing gaze – dead focused on him, never so much as blinking, let alone averting its gaze. A chill ran down his spine.

They made it to the office and once inside he breathed out a sigh of relief. The muffled noise of the factory was a lot more bearable here. The director, or so Loren presumed, grabbed a first aid kit off the wall and gestured to a chair by the wooden desk.

"Sit down. Let me take a look. Incidents at a factory are never fun, eh? I'll get the workplace injury paperwork printed out in a moment too. Gotta file it," he said with a hint of distaste while rummaging the kit for alcohol wipes and band-aids.

Loren shook his head, noticing the obvious dissatisfaction in the man's voice. He replied calmly. "It's whatever, just a scratch. Rather, where am I?"

The man's eyebrows shot up like fireworks, and he stared at him as if he had seen a ghost. "Uhhh. You must've hit your head pretty hard huh, Loren? You're here to personally inspect the manufacturing of the ITEs. As far as I'm aware at least," he swiped the cut on Loren's eyebrow with an alcohol wipe. The pain shot through his body like a lightning bolt, tearing at his mind and revealing his memories to him. The sharp pain worked like a catalyst for him, enabling him to remember the location and the jumpsuit that he was wearing. They were from his dreams, all of this was. A rush of scenarios caused a momentary panic and Loren fell into a momentary stupor.

"I uhh," he stuttered. "Right. Uh, Interstellar Travel Engines inspection, that's right." The rush of emotions and memories was displaced by another flood of pain from the wound. He winced and grunted, clenching his teeth. "Aughh!"

The man wiped a few more times and then pulled back, peeling a band-aid. "Looks alright, but might still wanna check in with the medics. Make sure you don't got a concussion or something. We need our lead inspector in good health and right mind after all," he pressed the band-aid over the wound and nodded. "Sure you don't want the incident paperwork printed?"

Lorren nodded slowly. "Yeah, it's fine. I'm fine," he lied. He could hardly focus on the words the man was saying. His mind was in disarray, racing through the memories that came flooding a moment ago. He tried desperately to dismiss the rush of thoughts, but failed miserably. A moment later the black cat, noticing that Loren's treatment had been completed, leapt up onto his lap and instantly curled up. Loren instinctively placed his left hand on the cat and stroked through its soft fur, his thoughts slowing down and mind easing.

"Alright inspector," the director said as he glanced down at the cat with a slightly raised eyebrow, before getting up to leave. "I'll get the upper management and bring 'em here. You just wait here for a bit. Grab some water or coffee. Help yourself."

Loren nodded dismissively and continued to stroke the cat for a few minutes after the director had left.

Factory, interstellar travel engines, inspector, director, it all sort of made sense. It was much like in his dreams that had plagued his mind for years.

"Right, just another dream. A lucid dream," he tried to calm himself, letting his thoughts out. "I was at my desk, waiting for the..." He jumped off from his chair with a gasp. "No! Wait... Impossible!"

The cat's claws sank into his thick, industrial jumpsuit, piercing it and scratching his thighs as it clung on for dear life, hissing in fright. The pain from the scratches focused his mind once more and he sat back down instantly.

"Ah! Sorry, sorry kitty!" He carefully picked the cat up from his lap and sat it on the table. The location, the scenery. It all made sense now, it was all how he remembered from his dreams. Except for one thing which was different. The cat. He could not recall ever seeing a black cat in his dreams. He had never had a cat in his life.

The black cat sat down, watching him intently. Just as before, its piercing gaze did not break eye contact. Not so much as a blink. It stared. Loren ran his fingers through its soft fur once more, and then playfully booped the cat on the nose.

"You are the odd thing out," he said calmly, eyeing the cat. "I never had a cat, neither in the waking world, nor in my dreams. You, little kitty, should not be here. Who are you?" he gave it a chin scritch and watched curiously.

Suddenly the door opened and through it rushed the factory's noise, accompanied by the director who was followed by three men in expensive-looking suits. Each was overweight, had neatly tended hair, and either finely trimmed or cleanly shaved facial hair. 'They could not be more stereotypical....' Loren noted in his mind and turned to face the management team.

"Mmmhhmm. Hah... That was a walk! Mister, hah... Mister Povey? What? Phew... ahem" huffed the first of them. Shortest in height and largest in ego, by the looks of things. They looked as if they were not used to walking farther than from their car to the office.

'Yeap, that's them.' Loren thought.

The out-of-breath man reached for a handkerchief and wiped the sweat off his forehead. "What ah, took you so, hah, long to... hah... to find us, Mister Povey? Haff you no respect for our time?" he continued to huff. It was almost humorous how out of breath he was from a short walk and a couple of flights of stairs.

Loren leaned back, stroking the cat, the existence of which was seemingly ignored by all others present in the room. He eyed the management team and then proceeded to speak calmly.

"Of course I do, sirs. You see, there was an unfortunate incident in which I was involved. I slipped and fell off a catwalk, and lost consciousness for a while." He pointed at the bandage on his eyebrow. "But, I assure you, the work on ITE is going as planned, and the inspection report will be completed by the end of week. I'll personally see to it and will present it once it is complete," he put on his best act, sounding confident and on top of things.

The short and chubby one nodded eagerly as he poured himself a cup of water, "Yes yes, very good."

A slightly taller one, who was holding onto his hat, glanced at the clock and then at Loren. "Will the work be completed on time?"

The director of the factory stepped in the way, forcing the manager to focus on him. "Well, sir. You see, we work a three-shift, twenty-four-seven schedule. Our men are falling ill and are in need of a break. We constantly have to hire new staff but, well, training takes time and effort. Pulling away the efficient and skilled workers to train up the rookies takes time, but with the quality demands we can't allow inexperienced folks to work on the engines."

The manager rolled his eyes, disinterested, and replied in a sarcastic tone that irked Loren. "Well, they'll rest plenty once the star blows and we all die. Until then, do try to keep the work on schedule, or we'll be forced to look for a more competent, ahem, supervisor."

The director nodded. "Yes, we try our best."

Loren interrupted the obviously one-sided conversation with a remark that put the director at ease. "And that is all we could ever ask for. Everybody knows what's at stake, and threats are meaningless in this situation, sir."

Shortly after the managers left, Loren too departed the factory. As he stepped out onto the streets, his jaw dropped open, and he marveled at what he saw. Meanwhile, his furry companion sat in his shadow. Loren squinted, glancing up at the sky. It was brightly lit and pulsing with auroras that were visible in the setting sun.

"A planet on the verge of destruction. What a marvelous sight, although terrifying," he said without a second thought, not even realizing what he had just said.

After a long moment of admiration, he headed home. Although he had no memories of the location of his home, his body knew the way. The homes were small, modular construction. They were obviously put in place as a temporary residence for the factory workers to cut down on the commute times. The streets were flooded by factory workers in a variety of colored jumpsuits. Some were leaving their homes and heading for the factory, others were heading home for the day after finishing their shifts.

"No joke, work never stops huh?" he remarked, glancing at the cat that was still following him.

Once inside his home, he crashed down on the couch. The cat leapt up onto the coffee table and sat almost perfectly still, like an Egyptian statue, staring. Loren stared back. No matter how hard he thought and tried to recall, there were no memories of a cat. The cat was an abnormality, or so he concluded. As soon as his mind reached that conclusion, the cat leapt onto his lap and stood up, placing its paws on his chest. It stared deeply into his eyes, and then a rumbling voice echoed through Loren's mind. Like a roar of thunder, it sent his thoughts into disarray and shattered reality.

'You are not dreaming.'

Loren jumped up from his seat and stumbled backward from his station, eyes wide open as if he had just witnessed the most terrifying nightmare of his life. Sweat beaded on his forehead and his raggedy breath could be heard meters away. His colleagues, scattered around the office, gave him disgusted and annoyed glares for interrupting their peace. Those that couldn't see him, got up from their seats and stared at the worked-up scientist.

"Ahh crap," he muttered, pausing and nervously proceeding to tap and brush at his sleeves. "There was a spider! Crawled onto my arm! Sorry about the noise."

His colleagues returned to their work, ignoring everyone else around them as they always did. He returned to his station nervously and sat, jumping at every noise while trying to comb through his thoughts. His gaze wandered the room until it stumbled upon the cheap wall clock.

It read 11:48. He let out a slow breath, trying to regain his composure. "Haaahh, damn." He tried to remember what he had been working on before seemingly passing out.

The folder on the desk, titled Time Disruptor Test Sequence, was hint enough. He flipped it open and quickly scanned the stapled papers inside, featuring complex formulas and calculations. Closing it again he leaned back in his chair, staring dreamily at the clock. Phasing back into his usual day-dreaming state, combing through his thoughts and memories. He tried to sort out that new dream he had, but the efforts were in vain. It simply made no sense. It felt like other dreams but different.

Once the clock hit noon, he grabbed the necessary paperwork and headed for the test chambers. Much the same as he remembered doing before. Sam's hand waving before his face brought his dreamy mind to focus. He stopped in his tracks and turned to face Sam, her voice finally became audible amidst the noise of his thoughts.

"Explorer one to Ernea. Explorer one to Ernea. Loren, come in!" she teased and then grinned. "You've ignored me calling to you for the past thirty seconds. You good?"

He ignored her question and raised an eyebrow, watching her let out a sigh and roll her eyes.

"Yeah, figured as much. You're totally outta whack today, Loren. Focus!" she reached out and cupped his cheeks with the palms of her hands. "Focus Loren. We need our lead test sequence engineer to not be off in the fairy lands of daydreaming. Not today."

He smiled wearily, finding comfort in her warm hands. "I'm fine. Just, didn't sleep enough. Nothing a double shot of espresso can't fix. How much time have we got?"

Sam released his face and shrugged. "How do I know? Between thirty minutes and three hours, or more. You know the guys in engineering, they're always so damn slow with the delivery of the prototypes," she sighed again and patted his shoulder. "Anyway, you go ahead to the testing chamber and get a feel for the situation. I'll drop by the cafeteria and grab you an extra-strong coffee and a muffin." Her eyes darted to his as she examined the weary expression on his face.

"Yeah, thanks Sam. Owe ya one."

"You owe me far more than one," she smirked and turned to leave, yelling back over her shoulder "AND DON'T YOU FORGET THAT!"

He made his way to the testing chamber. The thick steel door had no windows and bore a red sign on it that read Top Secret. Authorized Personnel Only. It was far too familiar to him, he frequented these test chambers. He scanned the badge and then his retina, watching the massive door slide effortlessly into the wall. Upon entering the chamber he was greeted by a circular catwalk that hung half-height around the center sphere. The core of the sphere was glass, surrounded by a

Faraday cage, and an energy shield that enveloped the entirety of it, humming softly. It was transparent yet hazy, like looking at something distant distorted by a heat haze.

He headed for the central station. A team of engineers had already gotten situated at their own stations and offered a bare nod in acknowledgment of his arrival, remaining focused on their tasks of running preliminary checks. A few quick checks from his side revealed no apparent issues or concerns.

Before long, Sam entered the testing chamber with a tray that filled the room with the pleasant aroma of fresh coffee and the sweet fragrance of a muffin. She made her way to Loren's station, where he made quick work of the snack and then proceeded to savor the strong coffee. It roused him from the dreamy state he had been in all day.

In between the conversations with Sam, he kept throwing glances at the cheap mechanical clock on the wall. The minute handle ticked again and it was 12:54.

The door hissed open and through it entered three men. Two were in unusual armor with rifles at their sides, and one, who appeared to be an engineer, carrying a suitcase. Loren glanced at Sam with a raised eyebrow. She just shrugged in response.

"Alright team! Let's get to work." Sam clapped her hands and jumped off the table. The team sprang into action.

She greeted the engineer and after a brief exchange, he approached the central station and input a pin-code into the keypad on the briefcase. It clicked open and he pulled out a cylindrical device, presenting it in his hands to Sam and Loren.

Sam nodded and then typed a few commands on the computer next to Loren's. The hum of the energy field ceased, and it slowly dissipated. A moment later the automated deposition chamber clicked into place and opened. Sam glanced at Loren who gave her a reassuring nod.

"Good to go," Sam smiled and stepped aside, gesturing with her hand at the deposition chamber to the engineer who was holding the prototype.

The device was inserted. The engineer who was responsible for the delivery of the prototype stepped back from the deposition chamber.

"Best of luck," he uttered.

"Thanks, hopefully that won't be necessary," Loren responded without averting his gaze from the monitor.

The engineer and the security team took their leave. Sam input a code into the deposition chamber and the device was pulled into the glass sphere.

Loren watched attentively as a mechanical arm slowly and precisely inserted the cylinder into an opening in the pedestal at the center of the glass sphere. Sam fed more commands into the console and the energy shield reactivated with a violent flicker.

"Alright! Let's roll," she commanded. "Automated logging, cameras rolling. Backup intervals - 30 seconds."

"Roger that Chief," responded one of the engineers.

"Chief Shiro?" Sam called out, glancing toward the camera on the wall, one of many.

"The committee is here. We're all watching, you may proceed," replied the department chief.

Loren's eyes darted to the shadows in the corner of the room where he had thought he saw a golden pair of eyes peering at him for a moment. He blinked, there was nothing.

"Nervous?" Sam asked with a grin.

Loren peeled his gaze from the shadows and focused on her. She was staring at the device in the glass sphere.

"Well..." he began.

"So are we. All of us. Now, let's get this party started." She looked down at him with a gentle smile. Her golden hair had a bluish hue to it as the light of the energy field reflected off of it. It resembled an aurora for a moment.

Loren smiled and shifted his attention to the monitor of his computer. Entering the formulas from the documents in his folder into the software. After all the inputs were done, he swallowed audibly and paused, finger hovering over the enter key on his keyboard.

"Do it. Fire up the test sequence." Sam coaxed, and he tapped the key. Leaning back in his chair, he shifted his gaze back into the shadowy corner. 'Still nothing. Relax, get a grip Loren.' His gaze rose up the wall until it reached the cheap clock. He watched the seconds tick by as the hum got louder with each passing second. He took a deep breath and closed his eyes.

"So, more weird dreams? Bad coffee? Black cat crossed the road? What's up with you?"

He jumped slightly at the sound of Sam's voice, startling him. "Aaaahhh! Sam! Wait... Sam?"

"Good job, you remembered my name. What's up with you? You seem, hmm, jumpy."

A chill ran down his spine. He stared at her in disbelief, his eyes wider than a full moon. "Sam? W...what do you mean what's up with me?"

He peeled his gaze from her and glanced around. He was sitting in his chair, by his computer, in his cubicle. "No... That can't be." He frantically searched for the clock on the wall. It read 7:13. "How...?"

"How what? How did I get here? I walked..." perplexed, she followed his gaze to the clock. "Yes, it can be. It is indeed only seven-thirteen. Early, I know. Why do you insist on showing up so early anyhow?"

He shook his head. "I uhhh... phew." His fingers dug into the armrests of his chair as he tried to maintain his focus and composure. Compulsory nausea from anxiety kicked in, as did the dizziness. He focused on his breathing, trying to control it so as not to slip into a panic attack. He stared at her like a deer into approaching headlights. His thoughts were a tangled mess. She returned her concerned gaze to him.

"Are you sure you're alright?" she asked quietly.

After another deep breath, he finally managed to exhale slowly and stutter out, "Yeah. I'm alright. I must've just dozed off. You know, me and my weird dreams," he smiled wearily.

After eyeing him for a moment, she smiled. "You better be, we need our lead test sequence engineer in the right brain space for testing the prototype today."

"Come again?" Loren's eyes shot open once more. "Today? Prototype? As in, the prototype?"

Sam let out a deep, concerned sigh. "Loren, are you sure you don't need a break? You've been so out of it lately. Yes, the prototype of the time disruptor that we spent a good portion of the past nine years on. And yes, today! In a few hours, in fact."

Loren leaned back in his chair, overwhelmed and feeling dizzy again. "This really can't be... and how did I, no, I didn't forget. Not this time," he glanced at her and smiled. "I remembered!"

Sam leaned a little closer. "Look, Loren, you've been working yourself to the bone lately. After the testing phase is completed, take a vacation, you hear me?"

"Yeah yeah!" he replied hastily, but it was obvious that his mind was elsewhere and he was no longer paying attention to Sam. He turned his attention to his computer, swiftly entered his password, and began to open various simulation software posthaste.

"Need anything?" Sam asked.

"Coffee? Please? And a painkiller, a big one. The size of a hockey puck."

Sam chortled. "Alright, hang tight. I'll fetch you an extra-strong one."

"Coffee? Or painkiller?" Loren queried her with a hint of sarcasm.

"Both."

Sam returned less than ten minutes later and sat a cup of steaming coffee on the desk in front of him. Squatting down beside him, she gently caressed his forearm and wrist. Curiously eyeing him as he adjusted values in the simulation software and analyzed the formulas. After a short while he leaned back, still paying her no attention, his focus instead seemed to be drawn to something else. She followed his gaze up the cubicle's wall and saw nothing out of the ordinary, yet Loren kept staring for a long moment.

"Oh," he suddenly snapped, noticing the coffee as its aroma reached his nostrils and pulled him out of his daydreamy state. "Thank you!"

"What's there?"

"Mmhhh? Where?" Loren asked, taking a careful sip of the steaming drink, his gaze wandering back to where he had just seen the shape of the black cat. To him, for the briefest of moments, it stood on the walls of the cubicle. But now there was nothing.

"Nothing? There was a uh, I saw a shimmer, might've been a fly," he replied, perplexed.

"Loren, I am worried about you. We can call off the test today. Go home, get some rest."

He turned to face her, taking another sip, and then shook his head energetically. "No no no! I'm fine. I just need to confirm something. But I'm fine! I assure you."

"Mmh. Alright then. If you say so. Just don't push yourself too hard, you hear me?" her voice was stern for a change.

"Yeah, thanks for the coffee by the way, but this is smaller than I expected." He picked up the pill off the table and grinned.

"Well, unfortunately, they already ate all the puck-sized ones," she smiled and got up to leave. "Alright, I'll leave you to it. Testing is scheduled for twelve flat by the way. See you then."

"Mhmm," Loren mumbled, watching her walk away for a minute before returning to work. When he swiveled in his chair to face his monitor, he came face to face with the black cat from before. It sat just in front of his monitor, staring at him.

Loren jolted back, startled by the sudden appearance of the animal. "Aaah! Good god. Don't just..." He watched the animal not react in any way, sitting as still as a statue.

Loren carefully sat the coffee cup down and pushed himself closer to the desk, eyeing the cat. Its eyes were mesmerizing, golden in hue, like the break of dawn. After swallowing audibly, he whispered.

"What are you?"

The cat remained reactionless.

Loren, deciding that it was another hallucination from his exhausted mind, reached for its head to give it a pat. He swiftly jerked his hand away when he felt soft and warm fur at his fingertips. It was a real, physical cat that sat there, staring at him.

"Not a dream. Not a..." a memory flashed in his mind. The memory of the most recent dream, the one in the factory, and the cat that he saw in it.

"Definitely not," he concluded. "What did you mean when you said you're not dreaming? Am I stuck in a time loop?" he kept his tone hushed so as not to disturb his colleagues.

But the cat remained silent and still.

Loren shook his head, suddenly feeling rather exhausted.

"Ahhh whatever. Alright. Gotta wrap up and then I could do with a quick..." his eyes closed as his mind drifted off into the land of unconsciousness. Darkness consumed him in an instant.

He dreamed of the factory again. As he woke on an industrial, metallic grate and felt the thin metal strips of the catwalk digging into his skin, he realized he had seen this dream before. He went through it as he remembered it, repeating events of the dream as close to his memories as he could. It still did not feel like a dream, instead more like reliving the events. The cat woke him from his dream in the same way it did before.

He awoke from his nap feeling rested and focused. He stretched, sleepily glancing around for the cat, but it was nowhere to be seen. Upon glancing at the clock, he grinned widely. The time read 11:48. 'I freaking knew it! It's exactly the same. This is astonishing!' he remarked to himself and then cleared his throat, remembering the events from before. Proceeding to jump up from his chair and stumble backward with an exclamation, he made the same excuse as before so he would not alter the events from his memories. After all, he desired to test his newly forming theory and explore this time-looping phenomenon more.

He reached for the folder and flipped it open. Tracing through formulas with his finger, he mumbled under his breath and crossed out a few segments of various formulas. He wrote down slightly altered versions in the white spaces above and below. Changing as little as a single digit or as much as half the formula. Based on his assumptions, these were the parts that determined the time of his arrival in each loop.

Originally, the formulas he had for the test sequence were expected to only shift back a few seconds, yet somehow they sent him back quite far in the day. He wanted to further explore how to control this and how to set the time correctly.

In what felt like days of restless time looping, Loren had come up with ways of manipulating the formulas. He now could set the exact arrival time that he wanted to be sent to, down to the second. For his past life's visions, he could only alter them by days or weeks, and he would always experience them in his dreams. The first half of the formula seemed to work in this timeline. The latter half of the formula, when changed drastically, would send him back into what he presumed to be his past life. A life in which he was an engineering inspector working on interstellar travel vessels, the arks as he learned their names later. They were meant to save humanity from the impending doom of an unstable star in their system. Yet the presence of the cat remained consistent. After a few loops, it was always there. Always watching, always waking him when he would travel to what he presumed to be his past life in his dreams.

He feared traveling back more than a day due to his concerns about having to precisely relive the entirety of the events leading up to the moment he input the sequence into the time disruptor.

Each time he'd awaken from traveling into the past life, the clock would read 11:48. His travels to the past life were always in the dreams.

Dozens of loops later, and still questions remained. Answers were more difficult to come by with each loop. As memories of past and present collided, they shattered his focus, sending his thoughts into disarray, and causing him to desire to explore more. He did not know what happened in the past and how he came to be in the present. He had memories of an entire life, complete with childhood and early adulthood, but something did not align. In the final moments of his past life that he got to see, he found himself to be the same age as he currently was. That was one of such oddities that he couldn't find an answer to.

He sat in his chair, tapping his fingers on the table, battling his conscience. On one hand, fear of traveling back too far persisted and discouraged him from testing further. He did not want to fracture the timeline and not be able to return to the comfortable life he was currently enjoying. He feared that traveling back more than a day would make it difficult to maintain an accurate replay of individual events. On the other hand, his curiosity was fueling him. He wanted to know why the memories of his childhood and early life, in the present, felt so artificial and not really there. He wanted to relive them again for himself.

He grabbed a pencil, gritting his teeth. 'I have to know. How did I come to be here? How am I here?' The urges and desire for knowledge won. He was willing to relive his life for several years, and even risk the timeline as he knew it, for the knowledge.

Having made up his mind he proceeded to change the formulas once again, estimating being sent back three years. The black cat sitting beside the folder reacted for the first time. The cat placed its paw on the part of the formula that Loren had intended to change next.

Loren glanced down at the silent, previously passive observer with his eyebrows raised, surprise obvious on his face. The surprised look faded, replaced by a frightened stare when he realized that the black cat was grinning at him.

Questioning his own sanity once more, he slowly pushed himself away in the chair, but as he pushed himself away, the chair moved closer to the table and the cat. Despite his best efforts to move away, he couldn't.

A voice that he had previously heard once before rumbled again in his mind, tearing at the deepest corners of his consciousness.

"Had your fun, human?" the voice reached the deepest corners of his consciousness.

Loren froze from fright and shock. It was a voice he had heard before.

"You've uncovered the truth that was to be forgotten," the voice continued to shatter his thoughts.

Loren opened his mouth to reply but his jaw hung open in silence.

"I have come to observe after noticing an abnormality in the fabric of time. You caused this abnormality, thus summoning me," the voice continued to echo through his mind, pushing away all of his thoughts, concerns, and questions.

"You showed no ill intent, only curiosity. As such, I allowed your journeys. I allowed you to explore, to learn, to see."

The cat's golden eyes did not so much as twitch as it watched Loren before it. The scientist's expression was a mixture of perplexion and awe.

"I am Ananda. A god, your species might call me. Creator of this world. As you have learned, your former world faced imminent destruction and yet your species showed potential. So I intervened." Its rumbling voice kept Loren's thoughts in disarray. Any and all questions he had managed to formulate were repeatedly obliterated.

"I created this world to grant your species another chance. To see what you could achieve under my watch and protection."

The voice fell silent.

Loren trembled in his seat, a foot away from the cat's face. He continued to breathe calmly, despite the shocking revelation before his very eyes. He took a moment to collect his thoughts, trying to organize them into a stuttering mess of words.

"I uh... your... presence... ex...existence is imposs-sible. Sci.. science denies... g-gods. The ve-ry i...idea of them..."

The cat blinked for the first time. The color of its eyes changed from golden to iridescent.

"You need not talk, human. I speak to your thoughts and you may do the same. Just think, and I will hear you."

Loren took a deep breath, mesmerized by Ananda's eyes, his thoughts in disarray still.

"Deny my existence as much as you desire, yet here I stand before you. You learned the truth of your past life yourself. You have seen it with your own eyes, did you not?"

Loren's mind flooded with questions as the rumbling voice fell silent once more.

'How is this possible? No wait! Was that a vision or reality? Have I gone insane?'

A distant roar, like thunder, echoed like laughter in his mind.

"Possible, impossible. All the same. Space and time, they work in ways incoherent to the human mind. What you saw was neither reality, nor a vision. It was existence, one that you witnessed."

Loren remained silent, yet his mind was quite loud. 'Existence. What do you mean? No. Okay. So it happened. Neither a dream or reality, it just happened?'

"So it did. It happened."

'And you are... a real god?'

"What humans call gods is not quite feasible. No one single being is omnipotent, omnipresent, almighty and unmighty at the same time. That would be a paradox, an impossible paradox. Indeed I made this world, therefore I am your god by definition. But in fact, I made many worlds, and yet I'm here, not there. Not everywhere, only here and only now. You will not understand, do not fret. Do not busy your mind with what you cannot comprehend. Not yet."

Loren suddenly felt a wave of calmness wash over him. His mind slowed, and his worries and fears disappeared. He nodded slowly and steadily.

"Each and every human from your former life is back, reincarnated. Your most vivid memories are of the past few years. That is the point of creation. All before, is forged. Yet many see their past lives in their dreams. Alas, no one is perfect. I could only do so much, for - your souls are so complex," Ananda continued to explain.

"Now tell me, human. Wish you to preserve the knowledge you acquired, or do you desire to remove it?"

Loren gulped nervously, realizing that this was perhaps the most important question in his life, in all of his lives. 'I... I as a researcher seek the truth.' he finally managed to line his thoughts out.

"Very well. So be it." Ananda slid his paw over the sheet of paper atop of which he sat. The words and formulas changed and morphed before Loren's eyes.

"The disruption of time I can permit no more. You had your fun, but alas. The test will fail, your department will disband in the coming months. Neither you, nor anybody else, will ever again attempt any sort of time research. The data will disappear and these experiments will be forgotten."

Loren nodded nervously. Sweat beaded up on his forehead.

"Good." The cat leapt off the table onto his lap and yawned. "You're free to write about your discoveries. The truth. The past. The present. The god Ananda. I do not mind you sharing the truth. Many will read your books, I assure you of that. A good career is it not?"

Loren nervously lowered his hand onto Ananda's head. The warm, soft fur was quite soothing to the touch. Ananda's eyes shifted back to the familiar golden hues. Loren chuckled softly, partly from nervousness and partly from relief.

"For a god you sure are pretty casual."

The voice laughed in his mind once more, like a thunderstorm in the distance. "And for a human, you are quite fascinating."

As soon as the echo of the voice dissipated, so did the cat.

Shark Filet

"Ah… yet another mortal, huh? How bold of you to come this far," spoke a woman, slowly descending towards a man that stood in the aisle of a kitchen below her. It was as if only the kitchen existed amidst the eternal darkness which surrounded it. It had walls and a floor, but no ceiling, and from that endless abyss that expanded forever, she descended. Her glowing-light blue eyes looked down upon the brave man, draped in chef's attire, who watched her with confidence brimming in his eyes.

"Greetings, goddess…" he spoke humbly.

"What stage are you on?" she inquired with a hint of amusement.

"I'm on the third stage of my ascension."

At last, she stepped down onto the sparkling, marble floor, and he found himself face to face with the goddess who would put him through his next trial. She stood out among the spotless kitchen where everything glistened and glowed. She made a few passes around him, scanning him, examining him from every angle, while looking down at him. Before her was a blonde man in a chef's whites. A classical and expected look. Tidy white coat, simple pants to match, nothing too fancy or out of the ordinary. She tittered playfully and hummed, enjoying how incredibly ordinary he was.

He humbly maintained eye contact but did not follow her with his head when she walked behind him. She was, without a doubt, a goddess, her beauty, and size, further confirmed her celestial nature. She towered over him, no less than two heads taller, and had long, light-colored eyelashes that perfectly complimented her faintly glowing blue eyes.

Her gorgeous red hair cascaded in waves. It was as if a playful flame was trickling down her silky, beautiful dress, that resembled a mixture of ancient Greek and Roman attires. Each fabric strand seemed timeless and eternal, each fold was graceful and perfect.

"Your name, little man?"

"It's Miller... Miller Monte."

"Delightful!" she exclaimed excitedly. "Now then, Miller, the one aspiring to become a chef for the gods. I welcome you to the third stage. A challenge is to begin, are you ready to undertake it no matter the difficulties?"

Miller turned on his heel, his long blond hair swung far as he did, and then instantly, he gave the goddess a courteous bow, "I, Miller Monte, accept your challenge!"

She slid her finger along his jaw until she reached his chin, then lifted her hand to guide his head until their gazes met and gave him a pleased smile.

"I am Canta, the Goddess of Taste. I challenge you to satisfy my desire for a perfect meal. Should you succeed, you shall have your ascension, chef. Until you satisfy my taste, you are to remain mortal."

He grinned at her, brimming with confidence.

"A perfect meal you shall have, your grace. What is it you desire?"

She spread her arms out. "This kitchen shall be your stage, but the ingredients you'll have to acquire on your own - from the land of mortals. Show me that you're worthy of cooking for us. I dare you to create a divine meal out of... relatively common ingredients. Show us that you are as brave as you are confident."

She snapped her fingers and a door made of light appeared beside Miller.

"I desire a meal made of shark as the main ingredient."

She pondered for a moment, then grinned - childlike and genuinely excited, "Ohh and strawberries for appetizer. I *love* strawberries. They better be perfectly ripe, from the southern lands!" her voice broke into an excited squeal towards the end, but Miller disregarded her enthusiasm and proceeded to calmly jot down her order in a small notebook.

"And, for the garnish? Also, any sauce preferences?"

She glanced at him and then pouted, mumbling quietly. "Don't care... don't know... salty? Something salty to compliment the fact that sharks are oceanic. Oh, but not too salty! A little salty. Just a smidge." Suddenly Miller felt her hand on his back. He glanced up from his notebook to see her give him a gleeful smirk as she pushed him through the door.

"*Good luuuucckk~*" she called out after him in a joyous, rhythmic tone.

As he got pushed through the door, the ground beneath him disappeared and he found himself falling.

For a moment, he closed his eyes out of fear, but then remembered that a deity would never harm a mortal during the trial of ascension. At least such were the rumored traditions and the supposed unspoken rule. He reopened his eyes and found himself falling, but the ground appeared not to be getting closer.

"Of course - she wouldn't just kill me. Alright, then... I guess... I'll start with the sauce! Salty..."

He continued falling for a while longer, puzzling where to find the best salt. "Salt of *Nayla*! I'll start there."

As if by his own wish, or perhaps it was, he noticed air resistance. He now realized that he was, in fact, actually falling - and at terminal velocity! But he was not falling straight down, instead, he was falling diagonally, to the West.

"AAAHHHH!!!" He shut his eyes tight, frightened.

Unbeknownst to him, he was rapidly approaching a small port town.

He slowly pried his eyes open to see if he was still falling, and he was. He noticed roads leading to the mountains on the horizon. There were pirate ships scattered throughout the port and the waters near it. He was certain that he had reached Nayla - a famous, pirate-ruled port city that was connected to the world's largest and finest salt mines. The majority of the world's salt came from these mines, but to get the truly finest quality salt, one had to acquire it from the source.

His gaze fixated on the mines that were not far from the city.

"Oh! The mines. They look so magnificent," he remarked and then crash-landed into a small barn just outside the city's walls. The sudden commotion alerted the sheep that were grazing on the field. The herd ran off while Miller slowly dug himself out from under the rubble - frightened but unscathed.

As Miller was dusting himself off and trying to recall the direction towards the mines, he was greeted by a farmer, that stood just outside the barn's door, the only thing that remained of it, with a pitchfork in hand. The farmer had a stern and annoyed expression on his face. Somehow it was rather obvious that the farmer wasn't too ecstatic about his sudden appearance. Maybe it was the pitchfork in his hands, or maybe the death glare he was giving Miller.

"Eyyy! Lad... why you destroy my barn?"

Miller looked over his shoulder at the pile of rubble, and then at the door and the barely standing frame of it.

"Apologies, sir. I am undergoing the trial of..."

The farmer angrily interrupted him. "I care not for your childish excuses lad! Ye'll hafta pay up, or else..." He glanced at his pitchfork.

Miller rummaged through his pockets. "Would if I...erhmm...if I could... Might I offer a fine meal, made from one of those sheep instead? I am a chef you see."

The farmer spat his weed stock out. "First ya destroy my barn, now threaten me livestock. I'll call the city guards on you."

Miller raised his hands. "No no! Wait, please, not the guards. I'm on a quest for the gods, I uhh..."

At that moment, the tall goddess seemed to unfurl from the earth, much like a flower that suddenly blossomed in front of them. Her features took shape, and she glanced around curiously.

"We'll have to work on your landing, mortal..."

"Excuse me, you are the one that suddenly pushed me through and sent me flying without as much as a heads up."

She shook her head. "Yes, well, you are brave and bold are you not? I'll deal with the farmer. Off you go now! I'm hungry. Don't make me wait."

Miller bowed. "Yes — your grace. I shall hurry."

The farmer angrily shouted at him, but his remarks were ignored.

"Now, good sire, my deepest apologies for the barn." She raised her hand, shaking it at her head level in a dismissive way, "Truly, what a shame that my little toy is so clumsy."

The barn rebuilt itself behind her, doubling in size while at it. The farmer watched in astonishment as the goddess, who seemed indifferent, proceeded to explain her stance, while the rubble continued to rebuild itself into a barn.

"I do hope you'll forgive me, but I must take my leave now."

With his jaw agape - he merely nodded at her in response, unable to utter a single word.

Soon after, the chef found himself standing at the mine, reading a sign. *'Salt mines of Nayla are temporarily closed. Entry is strictly forbidden due to risks involved.'*

He scanned the abandoned watch posts and worker posts. Not a soul to be found in the vicinity. He shrugged.

"The finest salt in all of the world awaits, no risk is too great... hopefully."

The growling voice that came from behind him quickly changed his mind.

"Hey Lad. I best hope you're not considering breaking the *'no entry'* rule."

Miller jumped out of fear and swiftly turned around. "SORRY!? Me!? Me not! Not me, no, never! I was just thinking out loud!!"

A few paces in front of him stood a tall, muscular beastman with a lion face, fur thick enough to shield from swords, and a physique that resembled a perfectly chiseled marble statue of a god.

"Hehe... easy lad... what cha so scared of? These fangs?" He bared his fangs at Miller whose eyes grew wider.

"What do you need such big fangs for?"

"To tear my meal piece by piece... I like a well-done steak," he winked.

"S... stay back! I'm..."

"A trespasser on my territory. An intruder. A criminal. A.... *meal*." The beastman snarled, sniffing the air. "You... what *is* that scent?"

Miller looked over his shoulder at the mine, contemplating his chances of being able to outrun a beastman. The beastman grinned.

"Don't bother trying. If I wanted to harm you, I'd have done so long ago." The beastman stepped back a half-step and smirked, no longer snarling. "So, you need some salt huh? Per your attire, you're a chef I presume?"

The sudden shift in tone and approach left Miller bumfuzzled. "Yeah... Uhmm... I need the finest of salts, straight from the source."

"I see... Unfortunately, the stockpiles are depleted, and the mines are closed for retrofitting due to a couple of cave-ins."

The beastman paused for a moment and then pointed over his shoulder at a hangar in the back. "Head there, use the tracks and trolley in there, enter the Eastern tunnel, **not** Western! That means go *right* at the fork. It's one of our reserve mineshafts. Should suffice, it's not very deep either." He turned to leave.

Miller blinked in disbelief. "Uhh... Thanks? Who are you by the way?"

The muscular beastman did not stop, nor as much as turn his head, he kept walking, while waving his hand dismissively.

"Captain Levi, my pleasure and so on, and so forth. Go! Before I change my mind."

'Oh... wow... he's nicer than the rumors say.' Miller remarked and swiftly ran to the hangar, opting not to test the beastman's patience. Inside he found an automaton, a mechanical construct of sorts that was standing next to a tracked trolley that resembled a large mine cart. He approached it with awe on his face.

"Whoaa... an automaton!? Never seen them up close before."

Beside it was a ladder that leaned against the trolley, Miller climbed it.

Once inside, he examined the control panel, which was relatively simple, at least - at first glance. It had a button, a speed lever, and a horizontal lever which Miller assumed to be for directional control. He pressed the button at the center.

The automaton buzzed to life. Its joints creaked and its body vibrated for a moment. The cart jerked, making him stumble and fight to regain his balance when the automaton began to move, pushing the cart forward.

Miller smiled excitedly, like a child on a rollercoaster for the first time. "Fascinating! An automaton-powered trolley. Truly next level. Must've been made by the dwarves."

The mechanical creature kept the pace that Miller set with the vertical lever that he assumed to be the speed control.

Shortly after, Miller found himself at the fork. A three-way split - straight ahead, left, and right. Miller shifted the lever to the right, but the trolley went straight...

"No! Wait! No! No no no no no! STOP!" Miller yelled as he yanked the speed lever all the way back, in a desperate attempt to bring the automaton to a stop. To his surprise, it only picked up pace and, shortly after, burst into a full-on sprint as the slope got steeper, accelerating.

The trolley shook, trembling from the vibration of the imperfect steel wheels on the tracks as it accelerated. Soon after, it reached speeds that far exceeded not only the safety regulations but likely, also the design specifications of the trolley. The automaton's joints creaked and squeaked in agony, like an old rusty gate that was being forced open for the first time in years.

Occasionally, a popping sound broke the mundaneness of the squeaks and the grinding sound of wheels as the situation quickly got out of control. *'Canta hear my plea! Have mercy on me...'* he prayed in his mind, grasping onto the handlebar by the control panel. He clung on for his dear life while screaming at the top of his lungs, but his scream was barely audible over the other noises that took place.

Metal clanked against metal. He glanced in fright over his shoulder to see that one arm of the automaton had fallen off, its legs wobbled uncontrollably, barely attached. The automaton shed bolts and plates with every step it took, leaving behind a trail of scrap. *'I really don't think any of this was part of the design,'* Miller remarked, concerned for a moment before a sudden and loud *thump* turned his lights off. Darkness engulfed him in an instant when a low-hanging sign that read — ***keep your head and hands down,*** greeted the back of his head. Miller, who was bemused by the self-disassembling automaton and was facing the other direction, was oblivious to the approaching sign.

The goddess let out a dramatic sigh in a comical display of exasperation and disappointment. She now stood beside the passed-out chef, shaking her head in disbelief as the automaton turned itself into a pile of scrap and proceeded to collapse in a loud crash behind them, destroying the tracks in its wake. The obliterated tracks send a shockwave through those still intact, causing the trolley to derail - heading straight at a wall. The goddess glared furiously at the wall. The wall did not dare stand in the goddess' way and parted itself before her, opening a path and forming a soft surface for a safe landing.

Miller awoke an unknown amount of time later, sitting against the wall in a cave. A small pouch was resting on his lap with a note beside it. He glanced at the pile of scraps that only vaguely resembled the trolley that he rode. Its remains were half-engulfed in a sandy substance, sinking slowly. Only the ground upon which he sat, and a path out, appeared to be solid.

He reached for the note and read it, then smiled innocently, and tucked it away. He then pried open the pouch to find a handful of coarse salt crystals inside. His lips curled into a smile, *'Thank you, Canta.'*

The first ingredient has been acquired, two to go.

He walked back up the mineshaft, past the crash site and mangled tracks, leaning on the wall to support him, as he tried to keep his balance. *'Best leave quick, if Levi sees any of this... he'll probably make a meal out of me long before I can make Canta her desired meal.'*

A few short hours passed, and he made his way out of the mineshaft and back to the town. Despite the horrific crash, he was rather astonished that he escaped unscathed, well, except for the throbbing headache. Fortunately for him, and his quest, he sustained no major injuries, and the headache seemed to be passing swiftly; each step he took eased the ache.

Soon, he found himself standing at the famous, pirate-ridden docks of Nayla, eyeing the various vessels and pondering which one to approach. *'Should also go for one that's sailing South, so they can take me along... hmmmm... Pirates... pirates... more pirates, ohhh merchants... the Empire's navy gunship? Gorgeous! But I'll pass.'* He marveled at the various sea-faring vessels.

"Pirates are probably the cheapest!"

"What'd ya say scallywag?" Grumbled a pirate who was walking past him, carrying a bag of grain over his shoulder.

"Oh nothing, sorry, I didn't mean it like that."

"Yeh better had not..."

At last, Miller mustered up his courage and approached the nearest, half-decent-looking pirate vessel.

A sailor in ragged clothes greeted him with a grunt, and although his clothes were shaggy, he wore very fancy, rich-looking boots. The sailor spat onto the dock, standing by the boarding ramp when Miller approached, "Ye?"

Miller attempted desperately to look over his broad, hairy shoulders.

"I uhmm... am Miller, friend offfff..." He wondered for a moment whether a lie was a good idea or not, "a... friend of, erhm, Captain Levi." He forced an awkward smile as he stared the sailor in the eyes.

The sailor squinted at him momentarily, before suddenly slapping his shoulder with enough force to send him down to his knee.

"Ughh!" grunted Miller, and then found himself lifted back up to his feet by a thick, strong arm that wrapped around him in a friendly manner.

"Why ye didn't say so right away ya scrawny bastard? Come aboard!" He released Miller and gestured at the boarding ramp leading up to a dirty ship.

Miller desperately tried not to panic. *Are they really that dumb? How did that stupid lie work?'*

The pirate guided him up the boarding ramp to the ship's main deck and paused to introduce the crew. A gray sheep stood in the middle of it - leashed to the mainmast. There were a few raggedy sailors in fancy shoes, who were minding their own business. Some were scrubbing the ship's deck and railings while others were finishing up loading cargo and checking the sails.

"Arr, we be the shoe-pirates!" the sailor spoke, lifting his foot and grinning a grin that missed several teeth.

"Look ye here, mighty fine set o'boots aye?"

Miller examined the fancy, fresh-looking, and high-quality boot and nodded.

"Quite the craftsmanship, matey!"

The sailor nodded excitedly.

"Arr now ye speakin.' We be robbin' naught but the shoe merchants, ghehehe. So, what the big Captain's friend after? Eh? Plunderin' some booty? Raidin'? Ahhh know! Seeking a grand trrreasurr aye?"

Miller shook his head nervously.

"No, no, uhmm... I ahhh... I be on a shark hunt!"

"Ehhh?" The sailor raised his eyebrow. "Ah... shark...?"

The rest of the crew suddenly stopped and stared at him. The sailor who greeted him squinted at him once more before slapping his back with enough force to send Miller stumbling halfway across the deck.

"Very well! Tis 'bout time we put the cursed sheep to a good use, eh, mateys?? Arr, it be BAIT!" he cackled.

"Got that blasted baah in exchange fer few spare boots we 'ad, but there be no soul aboard that can cook it, so we adopted it as our mascot of sorts, gheheh."

He clapped his hands, "Alright me hearties, we set sail in thirty," he commanded, "ah be the Captain of this 'ere vessel by the way, and yer guide, ghehe."

Miller watched him with an astonished expression. He was shocked that a man so simply dressed and mannered was a captain of pirates. He always thought that all pirates would be absolute savages, and that captains would stand out amidst the crew, looking fancier than the rest. Nay, there he stood, their captain, looking as plain as the rest of the crew members. The captain headed to the helm, prepared to set sail. The rest of the crew hurried to secure the cargo and ready the sails.

Miller followed. An hour or less passed, and they were now sailing fast toward the vast, open waters, heading straight into the setting sun.

Time passed swiftly and the night fell upon them sooner than he had anticipated. Miller cooked them up some simple grilled fish as a token of his gratitude and the crew relished the simple meal. He found comfort in the boisterous company of weathered sailors and found himself almost enjoying this experience, almost. If only it wasn't for the constantly swaying floor beneath his feet, that part was anything but enjoyable or relaxing. Each step was a fight to maintain balance.

When the sun had set, the water turned black. Nothing in the world can quite compare to the endless vastness and absolute emptiness of an open ocean at night. The moon's crescent reflected in the water, disturbed only by the gentle waves that rocked the ship.

"Me hearties, light the lanterns on the port side, this should suffice. Let's get huntin' ye slackers," the captain ordered.

The crew hurried; Miller watched attentively. A few moments later the sheep was tied up and ready to be thrown off the plank to fulfill its role as shark bait.

The captain walked the plank to the edge and then slit his hand a little, he dropped a few drops of his blood into the water and grinned.

"Aye! Ready the spears and harpoons me hearties, we'll skewer the beast and lend a hand to our new matey." The crew scattered to ready and arm themselves.

Miller watched as the captain returned to the deck and then glanced at two crew members who grabbed the tied-up sheep by the legs and carried it toward the plank. The sheep let out a panicked *baaahh,* but its plea was ignored and its efforts to break free were in vain. The captain took a spot behind Miller, who was leaning on the railing, curiously watching the events that unfolded before him. The captain felt something tickle his nose, and then he sneezed,

"ACHOOO!!" A mighty sneeze it was. He slammed his powerful hand against Miller's back, toppling him and pushing him over the railing.

"Aghhh! T'was a good one," said the captain with a satisfied grin.

A loud splash followed his comment. The crew froze in place, as did the captain after yet another nervous *baaahhh* informed him that the splash was not the sheep, but his new matey.

Dumbfounded and suddenly jolted to his senses by the cold water, Miller panicked and thrashed about. "Ah!? Eh? Ahhh!??? AAAA!! H... HEELP!!" he called out, panicked.

One of the crew members made a dash for rope, but the captain paused him.

"Nayy lad, fetch the harpoons instead and prepare fer a hunt."

The crew watched as the panicked chef thrashed erratically in the water, attracting sharks.

"No! Splash le..." tried to warn one of the crew members, but his captain's massive hand over his mouth shut him up.

The captain shouted.

"SPLASH MORE! It be scarin' the sharks away! We're COMING!"

Miller, lost in panic, followed the captain's instructions, and splashed more vigorously. Something brushed against his leg. His heart sank and terror engulfed him. Pushing himself away and swimming closer to the ship.

"Hurry! Toss me a ladder or something!"

"There it be," grinned the captain as he prepared to throw his harpoon at a shark that had surfaced a few meters behind the chef.

The shark's jaw was agape, going for a chomp of the chef. Miller, regrettably, glanced over his shoulder, face turned as pale as the moon. "CANTAAA!!!" he cried out.

At that moment, a bug flew into the captain's eye, causing him to throw the harpoon in a sudden jolt. It pierced a crew member's foot.

Somebody at the bow of the ship shouted. "LAND AHOY," and somebody else responded in an even louder shout, "AND A GODDESS AT PORT!"

What happened after lasted but a blink; the shark floated out of the water and splashed down on the deck of the ship. The chef suddenly found himself sitting on the railing, with the goddess' warm hand resting gently on his back as if to prevent him from accidentally falling over.

Her gentle voice whispered, "Amusing," and then she disappeared as if she had never been there in the first place.

"What ye waiting for!? Slay da bloody beast!" ordered the captain, trying to get the pesky fly out of his eye, "And get ye some rum" he ordered to the wounded sailor whose foot he had accidentally pierced.

The rest of the crew made quick work of the not-so-helpless beast on the deck of their ship. It thrashed violently and resisted, but no pirates were harmed in the slaying. Amidst the chaos, Miller couldn't help but wonder why Canta kept coming to his aid. This was meant to be a challenge, but it was obvious by now that she was closely watching him. With each rescue, his resolve to make the finest meal for her - grew stronger.

By sunrise the next morning, when all was done and settled, Miller expertly dismantled the shark. He sliced out perfectly shaped and sized filets from its tender, chest area. This was the softest meat, or at least, so he had heard. He wiped the sweat off his brow, laying down the last of filets in the pile for the crew to take.

"Yer done an expert job, lad."

Exhausted, Miller yawned. His gaze fixated on the glittering path that was drawn on the water by the rising sun. "Beautiful... Say, how much to take me down South?"

"South?" The captain inquired. "What ye headin' South for?"

"That goddess from before, Canta, sent me on a quest. I am to gather ingredients to cook a meal for her, you see. The last ingredient is perfectly ripe strawberries from the Southern provinces."

"Ahhh. Arr be damned... yer hitting on a goddess? Bold! Very bold!" He slammed Miller's back which almost toppled him over again, but he was caught by the very same hand that firmly grasped the back of his white jacket and kept him from falling.

"We be headin' South if it's fer Captain Levi's matey."

Miller smiled nervously. "Yea... thanks!"

"Now be on yer way to slumber matey! Ya be needin' it."

A few days later, Miller and the shoe pirates docked at the city of Laner, a port city in the Southern provinces. Miller was quick on his feet to rush off the ship, and even quicker to prompt a few locals on the streets for directions to the nearest strawberry fields, they gladly pointed him in the right direction.

Miller walked with haste down the dirt road, occasionally being passed by carts pulled by horses. His mind lingered on the time limit for the freshness of the meat. He had it wrapped up in salt-lined cloth to preserve it, but even then, the meat would eventually lose its juiciness and freshness. Time was of the essence, the sooner he could find the strawberries, the better.

Simultaneously, he also contemplated recipes that he could make from the requested ingredients.

'Salty... fin broth?, maybe fish bone broth... that'll allow me to cook the filets in any way and then I could pour the broth over to make the meat juicier. Grilled? Seared... hmmm... Seared! Yes, seared shark filets... topped with fish broth, lightly salted, nestled in a bowl of... goldened rice and topped with shredded fried onions! Yes! Excellent. I'll call that... Monte's Treasure Chest.'

Once he decided, he continued to ponder over an appetizer.

'Need something refreshing, Strawberry's Serenity – fresh berries with sea-salted watermelon cubes. The salt will bring out the sweetness, and watermelon's juiciness will get her drooling prior to savoring the crispy strawberries. Ideal!'

"Hey friend," someone called out to Miller.

"Howdy!" he replied instinctively, lost in the world of his own thoughts. He glanced to the right to see a farmer sitting beside a cart with a broken wheel. His gaze wandered the cart - no strawberries in sight, so he let out a mildly disappointed whimper.

The farmer picked up on his distress. "What is it, friend?"

"I seek strawberries of the finest quality," replied Miller.

The farmer raised his eyebrow at him and then cackled. "Ah, heh, you're in luck lad, for there's one right over'ere."

He pointed with his thumb over his shoulder at a field behind him. Miller followed his gesture, excitement washed over him. He disregarded the distressed farmer, and any concerns as to why the farmer may have called out to him in the first place, and raced down the sloping grassy hill on the side of the path, shouting his gratitude, "THANK YOU!!!"

The damaged cart vanished, and the farmer's face distorted, and then morphed into something divine. Canta playfully tittered, watching Miller run toward the field, with a childish excitement, likes of which she had never seen before.

He ran up to a post that had a sign on it, and from it stretched out a feeble fence, made of twigs and jute rope.

The sign was damaged and torn, missing the lower half.

Warning was the only intact text. Miller's gaze wandered the field, scanning for what he needed - strawberry bushes. The part just past the fence appeared to be cotton bushes, but behind them, off in the distance, he thought he could see bushes with red berries.

With not much time left for hesitations, he threw his shoulder bag over his back and leaped over the frail fence, being cautious to not touch the fence, out of fear of it breaking.

After a few hasty steps in, he found himself knee-deep in quicksand, being sucked in. His eyes stuck wide open and every cell in his body panicked, screaming for him to escape. Lost to panic once more, he hardly even realized the fact that he was no longer in the fields but stranded in a desert instead. He gasped.

"Ughhh! No! NO! Let! Go! Of! ME!"

He grunted, struggling. Slowly he managed to bring a leg up and take a step, pushing himself forth just a little. Suddenly, he was somewhere entirely different - a jungle.

"Whoaaat the hell!? Where? Where am I?" He frantically looked around, frightened and perplexed.

A loud thump echoed through the forest, shaking the ground beneath him. It was followed by a beastly roar that made every microorganism within his body scream and beg for mercy. Whatever it was, it helped shift his priorities - from wondering where he was, to - not wanting to be anywhere near whatever made that sound.

He took a long step, bursting out into a full-on sprint that lasted exactly three steps, since each step he took - transported him somewhere else entirely. As he came to a stop, he found himself back in the field where he started.

"Holy... what is going on?"

A glance over his shoulder revealed that he was merely half a dozen or so steps past the fence, and still had a long way to go.

"Alright... Alright... You got this Miller. One steady step after another."

He took a deep breath, mustering his courage. He brought his leg up, slowly lowering it and taking another step forward. He now found himself on the precipice of a cliff.

A gust of wind forced him to hunch over to maintain balance. At that moment, he noticed the breathtaking scene before him. "Whoaaa..."

Beneath him was a city that hung off the side of a cliff, and another one further down, at the bottom.

The next step transported him to a beach. In a corner of his vision, he saw a tsunami on the horizon, and then it froze in an instant. In a desperate attempt to stop, he lost his balance and fell onto the freshly watered soil of the field where he began this bizarre adventure.

The scent of wet soil and fertilizer instilled a sense of familiarity in his panicked mind as he struggled to understand what was happening. He laid still for a while, too afraid to move, afraid he would be transported elsewhere again. After a while, it became evident that he had to press on. Canta was not going to appear and save him as she had done so in the past.

This was the final stretch, the final push for him.

After he mustered his courage yet again, he tested it once more. After getting himself off the ground and taking a small step he ended up in a medieval castle. Another step and he was in the middle of a green grassy field atop a snowy mountain peak.

"Ohh brrr... Nope!" He dismissed the location and leaped as far as he could, and now appeared inside a spaceship that was piloted by an opossum, but before the pilot noticed him, he took another step. That one teleported to a science laboratory, the next one to another medieval castle, then a wooden bridge that overhung a volcano, a dense - fairy forest, a space station, and then a place that caught his attention the most.

It was a lush grassy field that was beautifully contrasted by whiteness surrounding it at the horizon's edge. There were gorgeous red roses that protruded amidst the green grass. Awestruck for a moment, he admired this incredible place, until he noticed a figure in a black robe. The robed figure noticed him too. Anxiety and doubt crept up, and in haste he took another step and disappeared, reappearing back in the field.

His gaze fell upon a bush of strawberries just half a step from him. Hesitant at first, eventually he took the step, and to his surprise, he remained on the field. No volcanoes, no fairy forests, he was simply standing next to the strawberry bush that he sought after.

A lone tear rolled down his cheek as he rejoiced, having endured this bizarre, albeit not necessarily difficult or particularly dangerous challenge, but entirely on his own. He wiped the tear and squatted down, the realization set in, *I've no clue about strawberry picking actually... Or any other kind of berry picking. How does one determine if it's ripe and ready? The vibrancy of the color? Softness?'* He wondered, tracing gently one of the berries, which was purple in color.

Beside it hung a pink one, further up was a yellow one, and down below were green and red berries. They were surprisingly sparse. He blinked at the berries in disbelief.

"Didn't know that strawberries came in purple..."

After a few minutes of contemplating, he looked up; as if awaiting a sign from the heavens, "Which uhh... color do I pick? And size?"

His plea fell on deaf ears, and was ignored by the one he had hoped to hear the answer from, Canta.

A sly smirk grew on her face as she observed him. Miller, to her bemusement, proceeded to pick one of each of the strawberries. Once he gathered all he wanted, he turned and marched bravely toward the exit from the field, from where he came.

Each step took him to worlds he could not even begin to fathom. On one world, blue-skinned humanoid creatures battled humans in mechanical constructors that resembled the trolley's automaton he had encountered previously. On another, giant bugs waged war against a human army, armed with projectile weapons. One of the worlds had superhumans that battled a whole fleet of space-faring vessels, bright explosions were seen in the skies. On another, he saw a black fox whose piercing gaze made him desire to escape as fast as he could.

There it was, the fence, at last. He prepared to leap over it, but before he could commit to the leap, he appeared in the celestial kitchen. The grime and dirt disappeared, along with his exhaustion. His outfit was perfectly clean, as was he.

Canta sat upon the marble countertop, legs crossed, arms at her sides, leaning forward with morbid curiosity.

"What did you see?" she paused, "actually, tell me later... are your preparations complete? I am *starving.*"

Miller hesitantly shook his head.

"Uhm, no, I need some side ingredients, such as r..." before he could finish, the shelves at the sides, and the cold storage - filled up with all the ingredients he had thought of for the Strawberry's Serenity and the Monte's Treasure Chest meals.

"You... aren't going to make me gather those?"

She smirked at him and got off the counter. "No, they're merely side ingredients. Now then, make me something truly unique and delicious."

She strolled past him, brushing her fingers over his shoulder, from the edge of one to the edge of the other. He shuddered at her touch but regained his composure in an instant.

"Just you wait," he remarked with a confident grin as he began cooking.

He prepared the broth: shark's fin, oysters, crawfish's shell, and other various ingredients, and set it on low heat before he moved on to preparing the appetizer. He washed and gently dried them, then cut them into halves and assorted them on a platter. He filled the middle of it with vibrantly colored watermelon slices that he squished gently to let some juice fill the platter. He sprinkled the tiniest amount of salt onto the watermelon pieces, it dissolved almost instantly, mixing in with the fibers of the plant.

"Amusing," she remarked, watching the chef skillfully prepare ingredients he never worked with before, and even make presentable platters from them.

"Have you not admitted to knowing nothing about strawberries before?"

As he finished preparing the appetizer platter and set it aside, he began work on the main course. He began by putting rice in a pot and setting that on low heat. While that cooked and required no attention, he put all his focus on the main ingredient, the shark meat.

"I can't explain it... It's like the ingredients tell me how they wish to be cooked."

Miller began searing the filet. Each move was well calculated, and the order in which he was preparing the ingredients made sure that nothing would be too hot, or too cold, by the time the meal was served.

He finished searing the filet and wrapped it in a piece of shark's skin that he had boiled in the broth, leaving it in the hot pot for a while.

His attention shifted to frying the onions and rice. At first, he prepared and fried the onions, then separated half of them and tossed rice into the frying pan with the remaining half. He fried the rice till it was slightly crispy and had a gorgeous golden hue to it.

The ingredients were ready. He grabbed an elongated oval bowl and lined it with the perfectly golden fried rice. Then placed the wrapped filet on top, pierced a few holes through the skin with a knife, and poured a couple of tablespoons of broth over it. Lastly, he topped it all with the fried onions and gave it a light dusting with the salt of Nayla.

Miller presented the goddess with the appetizer – the Strawberry's Serenity first, which she enjoyed thoroughly. The alternation of sudden saltiness, replaced by the juicy sweetness of the watermelon, and then the mellow sweetness of the strawberries prepared her for the main course.

The Monte's Treasure Chest in appearance - vaguely resembled a chest filled with treasures. The golden hues played largely into it and the dish lived up to its name. It required the goddess to unfold the filet herself as if opening a chest. She found this to be an interesting and hassle-free experience as it was just a single large slice of skin she had to remove. The meat was soft, juicy, and full of flavor, with a hint of saltiness, which was perfectly offset and extinguished by the fried rice.

When she finished her meal, her face was decorated with a pleased smile. She glanced at Miller who was anxiously awaiting her verdict. "Well, o' Goddess of Taste. Have I managed to satisfy your craving for a divine meal?"

She nodded slowly, "I dare say - more than just satisfied. You even managed to do so in an amusing, and entertaining manner."

Miller squinted for a moment. "Hmm? Amusing?"

She grinned at him playfully. "Don't worry about it. I hereby announce that you, Miller Monte, have cleared my trial and are qualified to move on to the next stage."

Her announcement distracted Miller. At last, he felt as if a huge weight was lifted off his shoulder, letting out a long sigh of relief - he bowed courteously to her.

"Thank you, my goddess."

She nodded, and a sly smirk appeared on her face. "Entertain me in your next trial too, the trial of courage."

He smiled at her, pleased with his achievement, and then he realized what she said. "Come again? A trial of wha..." and then, just like that, he found himself standing on a trembling rope bridge that overhung a volcano. His calm voice rallied swiftly into a scream of terror, as he grabbed onto the bridge for his dear life. "AAAAAAAA!"

His next trial had begun — it will be a story for another day.

Snakes on a Search

A tall man in a long coat took cover in the shadows. He peeked around the corner and then whispered quietly as the wind into a seashell. It was a seemingly ordinary, beige colored on the outside with iridescent features on the inside, shell.

"Jess, I am in position. Where are you? Are you ready?"

Silence... Off in the distance a can rolled on the street, pushed along by a gust of wind.

"Never mind then..." he muttered under his breath. He squinted, focusing on a band of pirates that stood down the street from him, just by the entrance to the pier. Illuminated by a single street lantern, they appeared to be discussing something.

"Aha... I got you now you shady bastards! And your shady plans!" he muttered quietly once more, his lips curled up into a confident smirk.

He ducked around the corner and tried to reach out to his assistant once more.

"Jess! Come in!"

For several seconds there was nought but silence, and then a panting, exhausted voice replied at last.

"Ah.. ye? Ye... boss? I got... a... ah.... a bit caught up in some...thing! With something."

Hatheris let out a disappointed sigh and peeked around the corner once more. The pirates were gone.

"Jess... We gonna have to have a talk..."

A moment of blissful silence was interrupted by Jess's dissatisfied and a guilty mumble, "Of course boss..."

"I've lost them. Meet me back at the office."

"Yes, boss. On my way."

As he pushed the door open, he smiled weakly at the placard that read *Hatheris Detective Agency.* Inside he was greeted by his homely and all too familiar office. A small open space office with a couple of chairs, a sofa to the side and an old, tattered but sturdy looking desk. He walked up to the sofa and then fell upon it, his gaze fixated on the dusty window.

"Say Jess. When was the last time we dusted?"

"Oh jee I don't know boss... a few years ago?"

"Uhuh."

He laid in silence for a few minutes. His assistant leaned against the table, absentmindedly staring at the wall. His assistant was massive. A descendant of dragons, commonly referred to as just descendants. His horns were sharp and front facing, which gave him a mean and scowling expression, and a strong, thick and scaly tail that could kill a man. Worth mentioning however that for a descendant he was surprisingly harmless, easily intimidated, and even more easily flustered.

"So, Jess. What, or should I say, *who* distracted you this time?"

His assistant suddenly jumped from the table; his horns got caught on the lower hanging crystals of the chandelier. As the panicked young assistant carefully untangled the hanging decorative crystal chain of the chandelier from his horn, he coughed.

"Uhmm... a...friend, yes, a friend."

"Uhuh... A friend... A FRIEND? Your actions were a direct causation for the failure of our investigation. What kind of a *friend* is worth giving up on a mission for?"

"Y... ye... a uhm... a bunny friend," he hesitantly rumbled. His voice was like a distant roar of thunder. When he was hesitant, or flustered, the growl in his voice surfaced the most. Hatheris always found it amusing how easy it was to tell Jess's mood and thoughts just by his voice. And although Hatheris knew that Jess was as harmless as a teddy bear, the baddies did not, that is one of his most prominent features. Such was the primary reason why Jess was chosen over the better qualified applicants. At the pubs his presence alone was enough to ward off most troublemakers and rascals. The second reason being that bunny, or well, Jess's innate charisma and likable personality. With little to no effort he could swoon any woman he came across, often being oblivious to his success. Such trait was useful, and Hatheris used it frequently to acquire information.

Hatheris grinned at his assistant with a sly grin. "Aha. Was it Mi..." But before he could finish his sentence, Jess abruptly interrupted him in a desperate attempt to change the topic.

"SO! BOSS! That uhh... the pirates... what of them?" his voice rumbled like an approaching storm. Business talk — Hatheris' one and only weakness.

"Yeah, the Black Lagoon sailed off. We got nothing on them, again... tsk... we'll get 'em next time."

Jess grinned and let out a relaxed sigh, having successfully diverted the conversation away from his side activities and embarrassing questions. He knew full well that she was bad for him, that she caused the failure of this mission, but who could blame him? Hardly anyone could resist her allure.

"Aye boss. So, what's next on the agenda? The night is still young, we could start the next case."

Hatheris lazily got up from the sofa, yawned and stretched.

"Good point, sidekick." He slowly walked over to the table and picked up a folder with a yellow tag on it, a *missing person* tag.

"We got us a case of a missing adventurer. A famed Nagi Sho... shhhh..." he flipped the file open and glanced at the profile. "Shokshu. A po..." he coughed. "Ahem, a dwarf. City dweller dwarf at that, and a treasure hunter... Odd mix... Generally, the city dweller dwarves avoid the wilderness." He scratched his chin, curious.

"Ah well, no matter. Supposedly she set out in search of some legendary cake not long ago. Is that all?" He flipped the document over to the empty side. "That uh... that is all we have."

Jess was distracted. He was intently staring out the window at the empty dark street, his thoughts were filled with Mia, the bunny girl he longed for. Her long ears, silky smooth fur that covered them, and her gorgeous silvery eyes that were like two moons in the night sky. Her hair was like the pure first snow that blanketed the world.

"Jess?"

"Cake!?" he exclaimed distractedly.

"Well, at least you heard something..." Hatheris let out a sigh and rubbed his right eyebrow. It was not a sigh of frustration, nor was it a sigh of disappointment. It was an exhausted kind of sigh, one that you let out when a kid makes the same mistake for the fifth time. One you let out when you just cannot find it in you to explain why it is wrong yet again. He walked up to his sidekick, rolled up the file and smacked him on the backside of the head with it.

"No cake. We're looking for a missing adventurer that went out in search of a cake, not cake. It's more of a potato we're looking for than anything else."

"Pardon?" Jess inquired.

"Never mind."

"So... mermaids like cakes, don't they?" Jess said dreamily.

"For the third time, we're searching for a dwarf! Not a mermaid, not a cake, a DWARF! Get your head out of the gutter."

Jesse rubbed the back of his head where he got smacked. "Yes boss, treasure hunter, dwarf. Got it. Where do we begin?"

Hatheris shook his head in disbelief. *'Why the hell did I take him over anybody else...'* A sarcastic smile spread across his lips. "Oh I don't know... How about a *bakery?*"

"Ah. That makes sense, great idea boss. You're good at this."

"Ugghh... Let's go."

It was the middle of the night, and true to their duty, the two loyal detectives were restless until the case was solved. Which could not be said about the bakery's owner. He was no detective, not a policeman nor a city watchman. He was a humble baker. A man of simple origin, that slept at night, as did all other normal people. And the last thing he expected was a descendant of dragons, and an elf banging on his door and demanding information about a missing dwarf in middle of the night. The words he said were far from kind or welcoming, and the threats he spewed made even the mighty Jess shiver.

What followed threats were actions —actions of throwing various kitchen wares at the intruders who so rudely interrupted his sleep. At first it was baking trays and frying pans, followed by heavier duty tools, like rollers. Lastly the deadly utensils were put into action, and knives began to fly. That is the point at which detectives decided that a tactical retreat was the best course of action.

"Colossal waste of time..." Hatheris complained.

"Yes boss."

"He didn't even *hear us out!*"

"Indeed boss. He was quite rude."

"I mean.... I guess, perhaps he had a point with the: *why the hell did you wake me in middle of the night you imbeciles*, but still, hardly a reason to throw frying pans and knives are your guests."

"I agree boss... He got me good with that skillet."

Hatheris glanced at his sidekick and then raised an eyebrow out of confusion.

"Jess?"

"Yes, boss?"

"I have heard of thinking caps, I never heard of thinking pans..." He tilted his head to the side curiously. "A peculiar idea, does it work?"

"No, boss."

"Huh... Then you best remove it, not good for aerodynamics I would think, might slow you down even more."

Jess reached up to his head and then slowly peeled a pierced baking tray off his horn. He glanced at the thin metal sheet that was punctured by his horn and let out a disappointed grunt. "Ugh man... I'll have to pay him for the damaged item now."

"Right... You do that, I'll go rest. Meet me at the office at noon."

"Boss, we uhh, both sleep in the office. There's no reason to schedule our next meetup."

"Your talent for observing the obvious is quite spectacular, Jess."

The vigilant detectives rested for the night after an unfortunate incident with the baker. At last, the morning arrived, and with it, news. A loud bang on the door was followed by a moment of silence. The blissful silence ended with a note of nonstop - impatient banging that was accompanied by angry cursing.

"Ughhh... Jess... do the thiiiaaaawnnn..." mumbled Hatheris sleepily from the sofa, as he turned to the side.

His assistant sprang up like a doll from the floor futon on which he slept and leaped to his feet.

Groggy, barely able to focus, one eye still closed. His voice resembled an amateur rock band that was angrily plucking at the strings of their instruments and incoherently banging on the drums. "On it."

He swung the door open and towered in the doorway, looking sleepily down at the short person before him, with a magnificent beard. It was a mailperson, one of the Dwarf Delivery servicemen. He frowned at the giant that opened the door and then proceeded with business as usual. He raised his arm up at his shoulder, palm facing Jess, and then extended it sideways.

"La-ha-yo-ha," each part of his phrase accompanied movement he made with his arm, "you are so screwed." The dwarf lowered his arm and reached into his bag, pulled something out of it and angrily groaned.

"Gah! Where is it? Hold this for a minute." The dwarf handed a strange round object with a string sticking out at the top of it to Jess. It vaguely resembled a Christmas Tree ornament, but heavier. Jess blinked sleepily, trying to focus his blurry vision on the object, it did not appear familiar to his sleepy self. The dwarf continued to rummage through his bag in a desperate attempt to find the piece of mail he was meant to deliver to them, or so Jess presumed. He waited patiently.

A slow, exhausted yawn escaped Jess's mouth. He closed his eyes for the duration of the yawn, listening to the dwarf mumbling to himself, switching between common and Dwarfish tongues.

"Akhare denara! What's this doing here?" the dwarf exclaimed in surprise and then tossed something over his shoulder. As he dug back into his bag — whatever he threw earlier, exploded with a loud bang, sending a shockwave of dust and street debris through the door at Jess. Jess was now suddenly feeling rather awake. Simultaneously, the loud bang was a delightful wakeup call for Hatheris who, after the explosion, dove down from the sofa and shouted.

"WE'RE UNDER ATTACK!"

Startled by the sudden shout from his boss, Jess turned around clumsily. His thick, scaly tail hit the dwarf on the head as he turned to call out to his boss, sending the dwarf's helmet flying across the street. "Boss!?"

The dwarf stumbled backwards, dazed by the unexpected smack. He cursed in Dwarfish, but his frustration was ignored.

"DUCK FOR COVER!" Shouted Hatheris, covering his head.

"Nah boss, no attack, just a dwarf."

"A what?" he asked, battling the ringing in his ears.

"A DWARF!" Jess shouted.

"THE dwarf?" asked Hatheris, perplexed by the sudden overload of information. Confusedly assuming that somehow, by some miraculous turn of events, the dwarf they were meant to find showed up at their door.

"No, **A** dwarf. Dwarf Delivery Service," Jess corrected himself, walking over to help his boss up, still holding the peculiar, spherical object in his other hand. Hatheris watched him with a bewildered and dumbfounded expression.

After accepting his assistant's hand and lifting himself back up, Hatheris dusted off and stared at Jess. "I did not order a dwarf..."

"No boss, I mean **the** Dwarf Delivery Service, not **a** delivery of a dwarf service."

Hatheris blinked, still confused. "Uhuh..." and went to pour himself a cup of something hot to drink.

Jess returned to the unfinished matter of receiving a letter from a dwarf who appeared to be even angrier than before, and now, also, helmetless, somehow.

"There it is." The dwarf pulled out a letter from his bag and threw it at the towering giant before him. "Take the blasted letter and may your day blow."

The dwarf lifted his right hand up in a fist and slammed it against the side of his head. To Jess's best knowledge, that was a very rude dwarven gesture for *may a rock fall on your head.*

Jess watched the small man descend the steps of their office and then pick up his helmet off the street and storm off angrily. He turned, closed the door, and headed inside to bring the letter to Hatheris. His boss was leaning back in his chair lazily, sipping on a steaming black liquid in his cup. The coffee's aroma lingered in the air, pleasantly tickling Jess's nostrils, that were more sensitive than a human's.

"Remarkable wake-up call Jess. An overly dramatic dwarf with a flair for mail delivery with a *bang*. I sure hope that is not your newly devised method of waking me to discuss our cases."

"Yes... no! Of course not, boss."

"More coffee! So, news?"

"Ah, I'm not quite sure, I just awoke..." Jess began.

"No, I meant the letter Jess, the letter."

"Ah, yes, of course." He carefully sat the spherical object that was entrusted to him by the dwarf on the desk behind which Hatheris sat, and then opened the envelope.

Hatheris' sleepy vision desperately tried to make sense of the mysterious spherical object that was ever so slowly rolling from the center of his desk toward the edge. He watched it attentively, entertained by it but too sleepy to make sense of it, or to act in any way.

"Ahem... Dear Detective Hatheris. This is constable Nyn of the City Watch. I am writing to inform you that per order by the mayor, you are to vacate the premises of your office, due to the following reasons: waste of space and city's resources. Signed - sincerely, Nyn."

As Jess finished reading, the spherical object reached the edge of the desk. Hatheris held his breath for a moment, watching the sphere come to a halt, and once it did, he let out a relaxed sigh. He nervously raised his hand and shook it with no real intent, but Jess interpreted the gesture as *look up*.

"An exceptional timing. I was just thinking of relocating somewhere more, business friendly... a house by the lakeside perhaps?"

"Perhaps? But what's with the ceiling?"

Hatheris just shook his head.

Distracted by the unspectacular ceiling, Jess took a step forward, against the table, bumping it. This caused the mysterious sphere to roll off the edge.

Hatheris watched the object fall to the floor, and then upon impacting the floor, it began to hiss.

"Oh... Jess, do you know what dwarves like?"

"Uh, gold?"

"And explosives. It would appear we won't need to worry about moving our belongings. As they say, travel light!" He then hastily leaped to his feet, and even more promptly jumped out the window behind him.

Jess acted purely on instinct and leaped out of the window as well, following Hatheris. A moment later, a loud bang shook the city block, waking all who still managed to remain asleep despite the earlier commotion.

"Well... So that takes care of the complications of moving offices. With that sorted, off we go." Hatheris dusted himself off, adjusted his coat and turned to leave without a care in the world.

The rest of the day they spent exploring the deepest, darkest corner of the city. And that is not an exaggeration. They ended up in the sewers, does not get deeper or darker than that. Well, Jess ended up there. Hatheris found himself comfortably resting on a bench on a bridge after demanding that his assistant fetch him the goblin king and his rat — for questioning, regarding the missing adventurer. Unwillingly, Jess fulfilled what was requested of him.

Although it took many hours longer than expected. He at last returned with a goblin over his shoulder, and a rat that sat upon his other shoulder.

"Back, boss."

"Phenomenal observation skills. Won't be long before you manage to correctly tell the time," Hatheris remarked with an obvious sarcasm in his tone. The sun was setting, it had been half a day since Jess left. He scanned his sidekick up and down, noticing numerous obvious lipstick marks around his face and neck.

"I see you had a passionate encounter; I sure hope it wasn't with our informant. Unless it's some kind of new interrogation technique I'm not versed in."

"Uh, no boss... Just ran into some... difficulties."

"Difficulties that jumped at you I take it. Glad you managed to escape unscathed, but not unmarked." His attention shifted to the goblin king that Jess was holding out by the armpits, not setting him down.

It jerked its body in an attempt to break loose.

"What a wonderfuls reunion, detectives," snarled a small, green skinned humanoid creature with a sly grin. A make-shift crown made of scraps decorated his head. "Whats you needs?"

"Keep the pleasure. It's all yours. Nagi?"

"Wrong! Ams not!" screeched the goblin.

"Not you. Do any scrap-bells ring when you hear that name?"

The goblin king cackled. "Keheh... Yes's. Nagi Shokoko....Coco..? Coconut!"

Hathers sighed. Jess lifted the goblin higher and stepped closer to the edge of the bridge. "Speak or uhh... I'll dump you into the river!" Jess demanded hesitantly.

The goblin squirmed in his tight grasp. "Noo!! Not waters. It will wash my stench! No I plead to you!! I remembers now, Shokshu! It was Shokshu! I'll tell you everything."

Hatheris nodded unenthusiastically.

"Right right! The dwarf with blue hairs, a city dwellers but a treasure hunters. She left... in searches of cakes," continued the goblin.

"It's as if you memorized a missing person file. Phenomenal... I was not made aware that goblins can read, but I'm not here to test your memory. You know more, speak up or you'll be made to sparkle."

"Kheee! Fines. Nagi has, a toy car."

"And now something useful, unless we have to add a splash of persuasion?"

"Wests! Nagi gone Wests in searches of cake. Three towns over, maybe... maybe fours," The goblin screeched, pleadingly.

"Anything else?"

"The cakes not that goods. Only fool believes the rumors."

"Uhuh... Jess, let's go."

Jess carefully set the goblin king down on the bridge's railing and then swiftly turned to catch up to his boss. In doing so, he did not notice how his tail swept around and smacked the small green humanoid on the face, sending him over the ledge and into the water. A scream and a splash followed, and were ignored.

"Delightful job, assistant. You really learned some exquisite techniques for informant and witness relocation huh? I am quite impressed."

"Thanks boss...? I mean... of course."

They travelled far on foot. The journey took a couple of days and was filled with remarkable encounters, among them was a black cat and... well, that is about the most remarkable encounter they had.

They passed through the first town uneventfully, and in the second town they encountered a young maiden who seemed rather fond of cakes. Lianne was her name, and she accompanied them to the best baker in town. From the baker, the relentless detectives learned of the legendary, massive, super dense, and incredibly sweet cheesecake. He informed them that the cheesecake was baked just further West, in the lands of Mido. The land of legendary cakes, one of several lands of legendary cakes, and the next stop on Lianne's agenda of savoring every legendary cake in existence.

The town of Mido was rather welcoming, and gathering information about the legendary super dense and sweet cheesecake was not difficult.

Jess and Hatheris rested at the inn for the day, going through their notes.

"Gnomes of the forest make the legendary cake.... And we have a missing dwarf. I would say we might have a case of *forcefully or voluntarily changing the residence without informing anyone about it.*" Hatheris began.

"Bunny girl with long ears..." Jess replied in a distracted, dreamy tone.

"However, there are rumors of shady ingredients being mixed into the cake to make it more addictive and sought after."

"Mia..." Jess moaned distractedly.

"And we know that gnomes are known to experiment with recipes, and there are rumors of them abducting unsuspecting sweets lovers, such as our missing dwarf. So, we have a case of..."

"Bunny..."

Hatheris nodded. "Your talent for derailing my train of thought is almost as blazingly apparent as your talent for observing the obvious."

"She isn't here..." Jess concluded in a sad tone.

"Precisely my point. Bed time."

That night, Jess kept waking Hatheris up with his mumbling about his beloved bunny girl that he was missing, quite apparently, very much. However, the task at hand could not be put aside.

At the break of dawn Hatheris awoke his assistant and they ventured into the forest of the gnomes.

"Jess, we're looking for..."

Jess's ever distracted and wandering mind could only come up with a single response, a response Hatheris wished he did not have to hear ever again. "A bunny..."

"Say no more." Hatheris gave him an enthusiastic but sarcastic thumbs up and fell silent.

They continued onwards for several hours.

"Do say more... I can't quite recall the reason we entered this forest."

"To search for... I... don't quite recall, boss."

"Once again you strike me speechless with your outstanding expertise in observing the obvious."

Hatheris's eyes wandered the endlessly spanning forest. It was misty, but it was not mist, it was dust of some sort. He sniffed the air. No allergic reaction of any sorts was observed in himself or his assistant. His keen senses did not identify it as an immediate threat. While he was perplexed about forgetting the reason for coming here, he did not feel trapped, and so onwards they went. They were confused, but enjoying a peaceful stroll through the gorgeous, dusty forest, nonetheless.

Rays of sun broke through the canopy above and illuminated their path. It was almost magical. The path was clean, no overgrowth, no debris. It was clearly a frequently walked path, with dozens if not hundreds of various footsteps decorating the dry soil beneath their feet.

"Hear that?" Hatheris called out quietly after catching a hint of a gentle tune, off in the distance.

"I do," Jess confirmed.

"Fantastic! I've not gone completely mad. Thank you for the reassurance."

Hatheris was an elf, and so his hearing was sharp. He could tell with a high degree of confidence that the path they were on led in the direction of the music he was hearing. He could also tell that within a couple of hours they would encounter the source of it. They had no reason to rush, they had to pace themselves, especially since they ran out of water a couple of hours prior. Hatheris knew that pointless rushing would only make them thirstier, so a moderate pace was the best approach.

At last, they rounded a corner around a hill, and just up the path they could see a large open field, littered with picnic tables, and a rowdy crowd. As they got closer, they could see dozens of gnomes, tirelessly running among the tables, waiting them, and tending to their guests.

Hundreds of hikers were spread around dozens of tables. Various species, large and small. The food that decorated the tables varied as greatly as did the crowd. From wild-caught game to freshly baked goods.

The scent that lingered in the air was truly mouthwatering, and the endless chatter somehow felt homely. It felt like visiting a local tavern with a rowdy, loud, but welcoming community, on a Friday evening.

Hatheris glanced at the gnomes that were rushing about. They vaguely resembled the city-dwelling dwarves, except they were skinnier. At the corner of his eye, Hatheris caught a glimpse of a rare sight, a witch's hut. Outside it, on the patio, lay a young looking, red-haired girl. Before he had a chance to notice any additional details about her, he was pulled out of his tunnel vision by a high-pitched voice that came from below.

"Gaaaahhhrreetings, travelers. Welcome to Gnome Dining. Table for two?"

"Almost as observant as my assistant. I do believe there are two of us. Unless... I've lost my sanity, and this giant next to me is a figment of my imagination, in which case, I truly feel sorry for myself."

The gnome gave him a chuckle. "Very well, come along - stay so long!"

He led them to a small table that was nearest to them, waited for them both to take a seat and then leaped up on the table. He placed two menus down for them.

"Here's the menu, feel free to peek at it. A waiter will be with you shortly..." He struck a pose and paused. Waiting for a reaction, but none followed. "Well, uh... short...ly? Because... we're short!"

"Ah, I see, you offer standup comedy along with the dining. Is that part of the standard experience? Or do we have to pay extra for having to endure this?"

The gnome shrugged. "Well, we try to make you feel at home!" He jumped off the table and took his leave.

After a hearty meal, the memory of their initial task returned, and so began the investigation anew.

Hatheris interviewed some guests, and even staff, and ultimately, ended up face to face with the gnome lord, an overseer of the gnomish operations in this region.

"Your... gnomeshisty? It's a delight to earn your audience. I am Hatheris, and I have a few questions if you're not too - *short* on time..."

The gnome lord squinted at him, and then burst out into laughter at the pun. "No shortage here, except for my height, hah! Speak."

"Indulge me, and tell me, what caused me to forget why I was here, until I had some food. Surely not exhaustion."

The gnome nodded at Hatheris. "The fairy-dust. Half the forest is covered in it."

"And what might it be?"

"It's our replacement for flour. Tastier, denser but lighter, don't ask me how that works, I don't know. We bake with it. Tastes delightful, but has the undesired side effect of a short-duration memory loss when initially inhaled, or consumed."

"Ah, that would explain it all. All, except one thing," Hatheris continued.

"Aha!?"

"I'm a detective, on the case of a missing dwarf." Hatheris glared intently at the gnome lord.

"Ah! Why didn't cha say so from the start? The dwarf in question I presume to be our new chef. She found our dwelling, tasted our finest cake, and fell in love with it so much, that she demanded to join the baking crew."

"Astonishing... I wasted almost a week of my time to find a dwarf who has become a gnomish baker. Well, I did get to savor some of the goodness, but might I ask to see the dwarf?"

"Goodness is worth it, no?" The lord replied and then nodded. "Absolutely! Not even a question. I'll take you personally."

He led Hatheris to a small open field, with a field kitchen set up under the open sky. It mostly consisted of stone ovens, all of which were spewing smoke – each was in use, baking a special cake.

Seventeen gnomes, and one dwarf, rushed tirelessly back and forth between mixing stations, ovens, and delivery trays, preparing dough for the next cake, pulling out the finished product, and sending it off.

Hatheris watched the scene before him with amusement. It did not upset him that the case had resolved itself, or that the case had no resolution in this case. There was no missing dwarf, merely a relocated dwarf that did not inform anyone. On that note, he took his leave.

They stacked up on some food and began their adventure back, although no home waited for them, at least not Hatheris.

His office was gone, and there was nothing to hold him anywhere anymore.

"Hey boss..."

"Hey Jess." Hatheris replied sarcastically.

"Uh, I was just thinking... Would it be alright if I..." He hesitated.

"You can think? Jess, you're about as subtle as a train wreck. No need to fish for words, fishing was never your strong point, you were always the one more likely to get fished." He let out a friendly titter. "A vacation is well deserved. I think I'll stay in Mido for a while in fact."

Jess's expression practically sparkled from excitement of vacation. "That sounds spectacular."

They received payment for the task from Nagi's friend, who, soon after hearing of the whole situation, ended up joining his friend.

Hatheris opened a new office at the city of Mido, offering his standard range of services.

Jess settled down with his beloved Mia, no longer eager to perform duties as a detective, but his background made him the constable of the city's night guard.

Until one day, they reunited...

The End.

141

Afterword

So, you have made it to the end of this book, and the beginning of my journey into the realm of printed words.

This is but the first set of Wondrous Tales that have bravely completed their long venture from the digital realm of online docs and game chat to the tangible world of paper and ink.

While this is a significant milestone, it serves merely as a stepping stone on this long journey.

The path ahead looks as daunting as Miller's quest to become the chef of gods. No less nerve-wracking than Detective Hatheris's uneasy case of finding the missing treasure hunter, Nagi. The obstacles on this path rival the trials of hunting dragons. And the challenges ahead will test my devotion! And even though the path ahead is enshrouded in mystery, just like the archives of the Grand Library, the results shall be as marvelous as the Snow Rose.

Yet in the end, many more Wondrous Tales shall find their way into the world - through my pen, and fingertips. For I am the dream-weaver and writer, and it is my sole duty to breathe life into stories previously untold. To bring forth that which never existed before.

Until we meet again, dear reader.
- Viktor F. Krown

Discussion Questions

Which story or stories would you have wished to see included that did not make the cut?

Which story did you enjoy the most, and why?

Who or what is the most memorable character across all of these stories, and why?

If you are familiar with the original stories, what are your thoughts on the rewritten / expanded versions found in this book?

What is the most memorable event or scene across all of these stories, and why?

What is the most memorable location from these stories, and what made it so memorable?

Which story resonated with you the most, and why?

Which character felt most familiar to you, and what made you feel that way?

Did the writing style change between the stories? And if so, did it surprise you?

Which songs would you choose to be the soundtracks / theme songs for each story?

Acknowledgements

I am humbled by the hundreds of people who have attended the Wondrous Tales over the two years. Without an audience, there would be no tales.

A special note of gratitude, from the bottom of my heart goes to my best and dearest friend, Lis. You have done so much more for me than I could ever describe. There are not enough words in all the languages combined to express my gratitude to you. You are the reason I'm still here; you pick me up when I fall and push me when I stop. Thank you. This would not have happened without you.

I am humbled by the help I received on this project, and I am ever grateful to everyone who was involved with the creation of this book, and this project, whether directly or indirectly.

I would like to express my heartfelt and deepest gratitude to these folks who went out of their way and sacrificed their valuable time to help with proofreading and editing the stories that you find in this book. Atheris Hispida, Cincin, Crystal, Full Ahoy (Ente), Leo. Thank you all. Your contributions helped me improve my writing and morale. You all helped make this vision and silly idea come true.

Special thanks to the people who stepped out of their way to give me advice and help me out with the book cover design. Whether it was several hours in a call helping me adjust it and trying things out with me, or just some suggestions and tips, their help was immense, and I am ever grateful to have received it. The book cover would not have turned out quite so awesome without their help and guidance. Thank you: Leo, Nyeps, Dmitrij Jazunov and Zeyliadt.

Thank you to the people who stepped up to help with this project in numerous other ways, be it through testing various things and discussing ideas, reviewing something for me, helping me plan, or undertaking tasks to help out. You lot helped me shape this project into what it turned out to be:

Thank you to Saira – for helping with the digital bundle and handling screenshots for the wallpapers. Additionally, an enormous, and immeasurable thank you for taking the books handling and shipping.

Thank you to Iaknihs for putting aside some time to review the book formatting and styling, and for creating 3D models of the book to preview it, so I could showcase the cover design to everyone.

Thank you to Ember for helping me with some formatting decisions.

Thank you to Rapuhotelli, M'iyu and Nagi for the help with brainstorming, testing, and reviewing the forms, among other things.

Thank you to Lena for the immense help with organizing this project and all the tasks that had to be completed for it. Sorting it all out, brainstorming ideas with me, and discussing what might or might not work. Additionally, thank you for the help coming up with the book's title, and with in-game house decorating, running the venue, and help with software / technical issues. (There were many...)

Thank you to Erik Redbeard for helping with the software and gifting me the tools necessary to complete this project, as well as assistance with technical difficulties and questions as they arose. (There were many...)

Thank you to Cincin, Crystal, Leo, Lis, M'iyu, Nagi, Ruby, and others for the moral support, and for reminding me to rest occasionally during the work on this project, and everything else!

A very special thank you to Leo. You went out of your way to help me with this book a lot more than anybody else — Thank you so much!

Another one to Zeyliadt for stepping up to help fix the cover design issues post sample print. I am ever grateful and forever will be.

A separate thank you goes to Presea Diamond, and M'iyu Fhey for making a very special and unique event happen, the Streamer's Tales.

A special thank you to Jeathebelle for agreeing to narrate a story in audible style, and going out of his way to make it happen.

A dedicated thank you goes out to all of the Wondrous Tales staff, current and former. Anni / Rapu, Atheris, Ashlandis, Luna, Lena, Leona, and Silas. Thank you all for everything you did or do for the tales. Your help is / was greatly appreciated.

Last, but certainly not least, a thank you to everybody who has ever showed up at the tales, the @◇Audience. Be it once, twice, just passing by and checking the place out for fifteen minutes, or staying for the full story. Whether active on discord or not, returning or only visiting once, I thank you all nonetheless: Anni Kedontaus / Rapu Riverstone, Ashlandis Kahkol, Atheris Hispida, Celia Lune, Leona Lucifra / Lucynia Leoktema, Lunamana Zhongxin, Lydja Kysana / Neiri Kuzaragi, Shinano Deviluke, Silas Amaren, Rick Jones, Aqua

Riverstar, Cear Redbeard, Orlena Frex, Tuulia Riverstone, Slathac Yorvasch, Yuumi Deviluke, Waldros Randir, Aoi Shikibu, Apsalar Tali, Bardessica Rabbit, Bunbun Bunnikin, Callie Vileblood, Cin Namon, Rosho Azalea-woods, Crashh Boi, Full Ahoy, Gumi Gumimi, Help Me, Kazu Miwa, Lily Luneru, Linesi Zeksrath, Bluish Fire, Louisa Clairmont, M'iyu Fhey, Lone Ul, Misuzu Takane, Nagisa Shokushu, Natalie Rosie, Nii'na Noire, Nith'ira Kaz'ior, Nith'ira Kaza'iora, Nynu Teez, Paresse Yonel, Phara Low-wasamistake, Phelo Nunh, Presea Diamond, Renfa Sonken, Ruby Zeksrath, Iris Dragonstar, Saira Malaguld, Satu Harmaa, Sendoku Roxxstar, Shachor Ente, Raewyr Wolff, Soleia Salandra, Stalinsa Live, Tain Teez, Velystia Moonshadow, Vodil Calmacil, Y'rith Tewhra, Zhadowy Fel, Abigail Osnatia, Anuzim Mol, Aurelius Kawakari, Auria Lynn, Caenis Drogo, Efina Aventia, Ember Ava, Grimmy Kc, Hank Dawn, Imania Wells, Kai Mocha, Kami La'luna, Kvasaari Catalis, Laby Rint, Lni Ninku, Lufia Obsidianschweif, Luna Nocturna, Lynsa Lasso, Lyra Gray, Machram Fashonti, Magnolia Laminya, Rheyana Yreth, Riseon Misha, Sylvie Lousefaire, Taeko Silverlife, Theophilus Charmanain, Tiothene Asagari, Waffle Paw, Xenon Khan, Yukina Isozaki, A'xumi Firn, Adala Amayoko, Aeosia Kuraku, Aima Aestiva, Alanis Ze'niki, Alesia Xur, Amelia Arkwight, Aramea Val'nthir, Argennon Veneficus, Arlin Hunt, Arsen Hysen, Artoria Alter, Asta'ten Elakha, Astra Volans, Astria Faewood, Atrisce Kaata, Awayuki Edakumi, Badr A', Baelroq Firenze, Baki Norengoku, Berry Fufumani, Blubry Ver, Bongo Cat, Brazen Thorn, C'rahna Aba, C'tadhara Sheqa, Celeana Targaryen, Chi Oichi, Ciel Duskbloom, Daisi Chu, Clytae M'nestra, Colson Yeager, Cythien Serranis, Denji Dragneel, Divine Strawberry, Doppers Sanx, E'myha Lynxee, Elaene Arkwright, Ella Namka, Emma

Lanco, Ender Kajiya, Era Divinity, Erinna Gunhild, Erzaa Skarlett, Erzarona Dragonov, Escher Ashbourne, Faye Gramarye, Faye Slayer, Feymin Lumifey, Fidel Katzee, Flower Thorn, Furiyon Darksong, Gae Bulge, Godrakk Silverwing, Gorbeljin Bairon, Gri'seo Shiramine, Hamburger Steel, Heli Tear, Holgorgrim Cuddlehu, Ildiko Saeren, Ilgo Tia, Izaak Alexei, Izayoi Travalier, Jamie Olive, Jamulan Gantulga, Jigoku Shinpi, Kadino Todarin, Kae L'dalis, Kairi Satomi, Kaito Draakah, Kaleilah Qivryg, Kalisote Lissmino, Kallor Iscool, Kariri Kari, Karyanna Gradan, Katarina Malaguld, Katheryn Sunflare, Kavo'wo Mhemti, Khona'to Khamazom, Kigoh'a Mhezra, Kiki Ze'niki, Koppie Flynn, Kotori Ko, Krea Morsdomun, Kusu Godefroy, Kuu Chelewae, Lady Catriona, Launa Mae, Leiran Naweh, Lil Chu, Liliana Sora, Lilith Demonheart, Linley Dragonblood, Lintharia Exiled, Livia Nightbelt, Loren Marteau, Lozzi Pop, Luce Aeterna, Lucy Shishaku, Lumisael Noblefrost, Lyca Ruby, Maholon Lon, Mana Runja, Mara Fosa'irel, Marcus Livius, Marielle Okuda, Masya Lianeh, Maurice Delacroix, Maya Mool, Mayo Lasagne, Me Huu, Melynara Remn, Mephiston Godefroy, Mikky Sacrosaint, Mina'to Kimura, Mini Linsa, Mira Miroa, Misusszu Smolkane, Momo Boarpuncher, Mon Naimaalj, Mork Malogaan, Nanako Fumi, Nanako Natsuki, Needa Mimosa, Miss Avantasia, Nephsy The'Staller, Nia Rose, Noxissa Yin, Nunya Bijinesu, O'rix Tia, Odina Waterfall, Oniichan Daisuki, Ophelia Warden, Oryxeor Leoktetor, O'kay Mage, Pinky Pink, Pizzapasta Moment, Poppy Hana, Pudgie Dumpling, Raine Clement, Raphtalia Amaryllis, Raven Velnias, Ravenmourne Lightbane, Red Nava, Red Sol, Regulus Draco, Rew Rewn, Rex Armstrongh, Rey Charbonneau, Roaming Owl, Rosa Lunara, Rob'yn Gelson, Rui Bernstein, Saria Goguma, Scy Val'kor, Shard Yar, Shayla Moonwillow, Shem Ek', Shira Yomi, Shiraori Ladywhite, Shorana Bridgestone, Shrek The'third, Shy Rose, Silvaire Montenbelt, Sinon Amayoko, Sippy Cup, Solaris Ignis, Sorocia Redgrave, Sotaria Vaelia, Sovex

Lihzeh, Spectra Phantom, Spicy Peppers, Squirty Berty, Stazha Wrynn, Stella Starshot, Talan Quartz, Tanni Goro, Tarabas Caelum, Tasan Veto, Theox Terrin, Thidious Soro, Toast Jern, Toha Green, Tomana Dawnstar, Tyler Alarie, Urtica Dioica, Valette Emberblood, Valira Eldaerenth, Vanex Arcadia, Veera Two, Vichara Norvndr, X'shion Yuri, Xatulah Walpurgis, Y'melia Shun, Y'senna Kushinada, Yemaya Harzhapan, Yes Eeek, Ymir Ragnvindr, Yoyozu Yozu, Yukina Isozaki, Zittiano Rhoof... and all others whose names we may, and probably did miss - a couple of dozen, if not more. Thank you all, every single one of you!

And of course. My deepest gratitude goes to **you**, dear reader. You, the one who is reading this message right now. I am ever grateful to you!

Each person has a story to tell.
Each one has a tale to share.
Every one of you has an epic to recount and memories to recall.
Take a moment, take a deep breath.
Your Wondrous Tales begin here.

www.ingramcontent.com/pod-product-compliance
Lightning Source LLC
Chambersburg PA
CBHW021402150726
47989CB00005B/2364